CRIMINAL ACTIONS

HERO SERIES #5

M A COMLEY

JEAMEL PUBLISHING LIMITED

New York Times and USA Today bestselling author M A Comley
Published by Jeamel Publishing limited
Copyright © 2020 M A Comley
Digital Edition, License Notes

All rights reserved. This book or any portion thereof may not be reproduced, stored in a retrieval system, transmitted in any form or by any means electronic or mechanical, including photocopying, or used in any manner whatsoever without the express written permission of the author, except for the use of brief quotations in a book review or scholarly journal.

This is a work of fiction. Names, characters, places and incidents are a product of the author's imagination or are used fictitiously, and any resemblance to actual persons living or dead, business establishments, events or locales is entirely coincidental.

OTHER BOOKS BY M A COMLEY

Blind Justice (Novella)
Cruel Justice (Book #1)
Mortal Justice (Novella)
Impeding Justice (Book #2)
Final Justice (Book #3)
Foul Justice (Book #4)
Guaranteed Justice (Book #5)
Ultimate Justice (Book #6)
Virtual Justice (Book #7)
Hostile Justice (Book #8)
Tortured Justice (Book #9)
Rough Justice (Book #10)
Dubious Justice (Book #11)
Calculated Justice (Book #12)
Twisted Justice (Book #13)
Justice at Christmas (Short Story)
Justice at Christmas 2 (novella)
Prime Justice (Book #14)
Heroic Justice (Book #15)
Shameful Justice (Book #16)

Immoral Justice (Book #17)
Toxic Justice (Book #18)
Overdue Justice (Book #19)
Unfair Justice (a 10,000 word short story)
Irrational Justice (a 10,000 word short story)
Seeking Justice (a 15,000 word novella)
Caring For Justice (a 24,000 word novella)
Savage Justice (a 17,000 word novella coming Feb 2020)
Clever Deception (co-written by Linda S Prather)
Tragic Deception (co-written by Linda S Prather)
Sinful Deception (co-written by Linda S Prather)
Forever Watching You (DI Miranda Carr thriller)
Wrong Place (DI Sally Parker thriller #1)
No Hiding Place (DI Sally Parker thriller #2)
Cold Case (DI Sally Parker thriller#3)
Deadly Encounter (DI Sally Parker thriller #4)
Lost Innocence (DI Sally Parker thriller #5)
Goodbye, My Precious Child (DI Sally Parker #6)
Web of Deceit (DI Sally Parker Novella with Tara Lyons)
The Missing Children (DI Kayli Bright #1)
Killer On The Run (DI Kayli Bright #2)
Hidden Agenda (DI Kayli Bright #3)
Murderous Betrayal (Kayli Bright #4)
Dying Breath (Kayli Bright #5)
Taken (Kayli Bright #6 coming March 2020)
The Hostage Takers (DI Kayli Bright Novella)
No Right to Kill (DI Sara Ramsey #1)
Killer Blow (DI Sara Ramsey #2)
The Dead Can't Speak (DI Sara Ramsey #3)
Deluded (DI Sara Ramsey #4)
The Murder Pact (DI Sara Ramsey #5)
Twisted Revenge (DI Sara Ramsey #6 coming February 2020)
The Caller (co-written with Tara Lyons)
Evil In Disguise – a novel based on True events
Deadly Act (Hero series novella)

Torn Apart (Hero series #1)
End Result (Hero series #2)
In Plain Sight (Hero Series #3)
Double Jeopardy (Hero Series #4)
Criminal Actions (Hero Series #5)
Sole Intention (Intention series #1)
Grave Intention (Intention series #2)
Devious Intention (Intention #3)
Merry Widow (A Lorne Simpkins short story)
It's A Dog's Life (A Lorne Simpkins short story)
A Time To Heal (A Sweet Romance)
A Time For Change (A Sweet Romance)
High Spirits
The Temptation series (Romantic Suspense/New Adult Novellas)
Past Temptation
Lost Temptation
Cozy Mystery Series
Murder at the Wedding
Murder at the Hotel
Murder by the Sea
Tempting Christa (A billionaire romantic suspense co-authored by Tracie Delaney #1)
Avenging Christa (A billionaire romantic suspense co-authored by Tracie Delaney #2)

ACKNOWLEDGEMENTS

Thank you as always to my rock, Jean, I'd be lost without you in my life.

Special thanks as always go to @studioenp for their superb cover design expertise.

My heartfelt thanks go to my wonderful editor Emmy Ellis, my proofreaders Joseph, Barbara and Jacqueline for spotting all the lingering nits.

Thank you to Annette for allowing me to use your name in this book.

A very special shoutout to Sarah Hardy and her amazing team of helpful bloggers involved in the blog tour.

To Mary, gone, but never forgotten. I hope you found the peace you were searching for my dear friend.

KEEP IN TOUCH WITH THE AUTHOR

Twitter
https://twitter.com/Melcom1

Blog
http://melcomley.blogspot.com

Newsletter
http://smarturl.it/8jtcvv

BookBub
www.bookbub.com/authors/m-a-comley

1

Jacinda Meredith raced home from the park with the two children she cared for, April, five years old, and Willow, four. They were dragging their feet and ultimately raising her stress levels at the same time.

"Please, children, try and hurry. I promise there will be a bowl of ice cream at the end of it for both of you."

She hated bribing them. This was becoming a daily habit now, one that she detested, although it appeared to have the desired effect—the children upped their pace. She loved the little rascals to pieces, their funny expressions and the quirky way they spoke to her; however, with each passing day, they were becoming more and more expert at finding ways of ticking her off. She rarely showed any anxiety in their presence as she knew, after speaking to other nannies at the park, what a nightmare that would bring in the future. Kids had a sixth sense where feelings were concerned. One slip-up and they would pounce right away. Therefore, she was extra cautious in keeping her tone light with a slight smile stitched in place at all times when she was with them.

They rounded the corner of the street where they lived.

"Yay, Daddy's home," Willow shouted and, breaking free of her hand, he raced ahead.

"Be careful, Willow, don't run into the road," Jacinda called after him.

"He won't, don't worry," April said, looking up at her and giving Jacinda one of her toothy, reassuring smiles.

She ruffled April's hair. "He's distracted, anything could happen."

"There's Daddy now." April pointed ahead of them.

Jacinda's heart was in her mouth. She knew what lay ahead of her. The recriminations would come thick and fast once the children were safely tucked away in their playroom. *Why hadn't I clung to Willow's hand tighter? Why did he have to be like a whippet and take off like that?*

She gulped down the bile filling her throat and ensured her smile was set in place for when she entered the front door.

"Willow, what have I told you about running off like that?" Leonard Knox scolded his son.

"I'm sorry, Daddy. I won't do it again, I pwomise."

Jacinda was aware of what was coming next.

"I'll see you in my study after you've dealt with the children's needs, Jacinda."

"Yes, Mr Knox," she replied, fear tearing at her gut.

In spite of that, she saw to the children, took them into the kitchen and sat them at the table with a glass of milk and a small bowl of ice cream as she had promised. Her nerves mounted. She watched April and Willow wolf down the ice cream and leave the table. They raced through the house into their playroom at the front and played noisily for the next half an hour until Mr Knox ordered them to keep the noise down. Jacinda was sitting in the chair positioned in the bay window with one eye on the children and the other on people coming and going in the street outside. She was envious of their freedom. She had none.

Because she was caught up in her daydreaming, she neglected to hear Mr Knox enter the room. His bellow almost sent her hurtling skywards.

"I'm sorry. I'll make sure they keep the noise down, sir."

"Just do your job, that's all I ask. I have an important meeting I need to prepare for in the morning. I can't do that with all this commotion going on." He glared at her and marched out of the room.

It was evident he blamed her for the way the children were behaving. *I can't win...I've never been able to win. I hate it here, but I'm stuck. For me, there is no escape.*

Busy wallowing in her own self-pity, she failed to see Willow put a tiny bead in his mouth. His choking sent chills down her spine. April screamed, and Jacinda shot across the room. She hauled Willow to his feet and thumped the middle of his back with the heel of her hand. It took a few attempts to dislodge the offending item, but she was relieved to see the bead emerge and end up on the floor in front of them.

Mr Knox appeared in the doorway. "What the hell is going on in here? I thought I told you to control the children."

"Daddy, it's Willow. Jacundy just saved him," April announced, still unable to pronounce the nanny's name properly.

Mr Knox dropped to his knees to hug his son. "Willow, are you all right?"

The poor boy's eyes glistened with unshed tears. "Yes, Daddy. I think so."

Knox turned to Jacinda. "What happened?" he demanded, his eyes narrowing with contempt.

She picked up the bead his son had spat out moments earlier and held it in the palm of her hand. "He swallowed this."

"He *what*? How? You should've been watching him instead of staring out of the window. We pay you to care for our children. If you're not interested in doing that then I suggest you pack your bags right now, you hear me?"

Her head bowed, mortified, she replied, "I'm sorry, sir. I don't want to leave. I love working here. It won't happen again, sir, I give you my word."

The front door slammed, and Sadie Knox stood in the doorway of the room and peered over her husband's shoulder. "Leonard, what's going on here?"

"Willow swallowed something. He's all right now. I need you to look after the children while I sort this."

"I've just come home from work. I need to get out of my suit first. Anyway, that's why we pay her, to look after the kids."

Mr Knox tutted, an irritated expression appearing on his features. "Do what you have to do. I need to have a proper chat with Jacinda, it's urgent."

"Ah, I see. Okay, give me ten minutes to get changed. Jacinda, go make me a coffee if I've got to do your job for you."

She nodded and squeezed past the couple to get to the kitchen.

"Stop, take the children with you," Mrs Knox ordered angrily. "They should never be left alone, you hear me?"

"Yes, Mrs Knox. I'm so sorry, it won't happen again."

"Make sure you stick to your word about that in the future," she retorted harshly.

"I will. Come, April and Willow, into the kitchen."

The children each took one of her hands, and the three of them marched through the house. She felt relieved that Willow had pushed aside his bad experience. The raised voices of the children's parents crackled behind them. She tried to shut the argument out; however, she soon found herself straining her neck, trying to listen to what was being said. The conversation ended with Mrs Knox storming upstairs. Her heavy feet thumped in the master bedroom above.

Jacinda boiled the kettle and made two cups of coffee, one each for Sadie and Leonard. She enticed April and Willow back to the playroom and carried the tray containing the cups and saucers. Mr Knox was still standing in the doorway. He backed up to let Jacinda and the children past, his gaze intense, studying her. Her hands shook, and the cups rattled in their saucers.

He relieved her of the tray and walked into his study. Mrs Knox descended the stairs and glared at her, but once she entered the playroom with the children, a smile appeared on her face. Jacinda nipped into the study to retrieve Mrs Knox's coffee and placed it on the mantelpiece for her, then she left the room again and joined Mr Knox in his study.

"Close the door and lock it," he ordered.

Jacinda did as she was instructed. She shut her eyes and gulped down the saliva that was now residing in her mouth. "I'm sorry. Please forgive me, it won't happen again, sir."

"I *know* it won't. This is your final warning. For now, you will accept your punishment. Take your clothes off."

"But…sir…please, I'm begging you, don't do this."

"It is not open for discussion. Take off your clothes, *now*," he lowered his voice and sneered at her.

She knew there was no way he'd let her leave the room. She had to do what he wanted. Jacinda pulled her jumper over her head and removed her blouse. Each movement was filled with pain; she already had substantial bruises on her body from her past experiences of being alone with this man. His wife was fully aware of the situation and often encouraged it from the sidelines.

He stared at her, a warped smile tugging at the corners of his mouth. She slipped out of her jeans and stood before him, in her underwear. He tilted his head and clicked his fingers, instructing her to remove the rest.

"Please, I don't want to do this. Not again."

He shot across the room and gripped her around the throat. She spluttered, struggling to find a breath.

"You'll do as I want, *when* I want it, got that?"

She nodded. It was only a slight nod as her head movements were restricted by his grasp. Eventually, he removed his hand and stood back to watch as she tore off her knickers and her bra. Standing naked before him, she gulped several times. She tried to shield her modesty with her hands until he shook his head, silently warning her what would happen if she pissed him off further.

His gaze roamed her body, seemingly ignoring the bruises he and his wife had given her. She felt repulsed, used and dirty beyond words. *How did I get into this mess? I should have taken off the first time they attacked me. It's only escalated since then.*

"I can see the cogs in that little mind of yours churning. What are you thinking? Tell me your deepest and darkest secrets? Tell me what you want me to do to you?"

There was no way she could reveal the truth of how much she despised him. Instead, she smiled slightly, pretending to be shy. It was all a game to him, and now she had learnt to play along with that game, too. It was the only way to stay alive. It hadn't taken her long to figure that out. The first time he and his wife had beaten her, she'd spent the next forty-eight hours in bed. Not only wallowing in self-pity but also because they'd broken her arm and had refused to take her to the hospital. They'd strapped it up for her. Now it was deformed and the reason why she no longer wore T-shirts in the summer.

"I have no thoughts. All I have is regrets," she mumbled.

He placed a finger under her chin, forcing her to look at him. "Regrets? What kind of regrets?"

"For not keeping a proper eye on the children. It was my fault Willow almost choked today."

"On that we agree. Therefore, you can expect the punishment to be worse than any you've received before. Bend over the desk."

She tentatively walked to the other side of the large room, hesitating a moment while she said a silent prayer to God to keep her safe, something He'd neglected to do in the past.

His hands clutched her arm, squeezed the largest of her bruises, and he forced her to bend over. Her head touched the desk with a thud. She heard him disrobing behind her, all too aware of what was to come. He grunted and kicked off his trousers. His hands touched the cheeks of her backside, moulding and caressing her skin. The gentle movements didn't last for long. Soon the pummelling began, and this gave way to vicious slaps. She placed her fist in her mouth, aware that the punishment he would mete out would be a darn sight worse if she cried out, or even considered screaming.

He rammed himself into her then, thrusting away like an eager teenager getting laid for the first time. She resisted the urge to fight, transfixed by the bin in the corner of the room as her thoughts lay elsewhere. Scotland, her beautiful Scotland. If only she had remained up there with her parents, instead of travelling where the work was in Manchester. Boy, every night since her arrival, she'd regretted her foolhardiness to seek out pastures new. The grass wasn't always greener, was it? She'd learnt that the hard way—she was still learning it.

Thankfully, the man had very little stamina. After the deed was done, he always whispered in her ear that it was her fault. She excited him too much and that was the result. Utter bullshit, she knew that. Nonetheless, she was filled with relief when he began dressing again. She remained in situ until ordered to do otherwise. No doubt his gaze was trained on her body. She swallowed down the bile threatening to emerge.

Once he was dressed, he ordered her to stand. Aware of what was coming next, she closed her eyes and inhaled a large breath. The lashings with his belt struck her arms and legs. He ensured he never hit her face or hands, avoiding any unnecessary questions when she was out with the children. Again, her fist was rammed into her mouth, suppressing her cries.

"How dare you disrespect me and my family? You will do what you're paid to do and care for April and Willow properly in the future, do you hear me?"

She nodded.

He yanked her fist out of her mouth. "I didn't hear you."

"I will endeavour to put the children first at all times. I will never let you down again."

He nodded and, his eyes blazing with anger, he continued to thrash her. There was no point in objecting, she knew how long the punishment would take. All she had to do was hang on, to dig deep for survival.

Five minutes passed, although it seemed more like half an hour, but the clock on the wall confirmed the truth.

"Get dressed and get out of my sight. You make me physically sick," he said through gritted teeth.

Her body was crying out in pain, every movement far worse than the last. She had no idea how she was going to survive living with these people. The beatings were coming far more frequently now—every time the children messed up, she got the blame. They were too young to understand how to behave properly. She had pleaded with them on numerous occasions, but they were only four and five. Kids of that age always misbehaved, didn't they?

He watched her dress and then unlocked the door and held it open for her to leave.

"Thank you," she muttered. If she hadn't, he would have locked the door again and repeated his punishment.

She dug deep and summoned up a smile and entered the playroom. Mrs Knox narrowed her eyes and stared at her.

Jacinda nodded. "I can resume my duties now that your husband has ensured I have seen the errors of my ways, madam." It was the same response she delivered every time, the response they insisted she use.

"Mummy is going to get on with dinner now, sweethearts. Play nicely for Jacinda, won't you?"

"Yes, Mummy," April replied.

Her brother was far too distracted building the Lego car his father had bought him a while before to answer.

As she passed by, Mrs Knox growled at Jacinda. She stepped back, cowering from the woman's obvious hatred of her.

Alone with April and Willow, she felt safe once more. *How has it come to this?* She adored looking after the children, it was the rest of it she abhorred. The feelings of worthlessness that kept her awake at night. She couldn't remember the last time she had slept a full eight hours. Maybe if she had, it would ensure she was less likely to make the kind of mistakes that led to the humiliating punishments.

She watched the children play nicely for the next hour, until Mrs Knox called them for their dinner. Jacinda stood back then. Mrs Knox had always insisted that the evening meal was family time and didn't include her. Her dinner always consisted of what Mrs Knox deemed she was worth. Sometimes that meant she had a small portion of leftovers, but more often than not, it only meant her total calories for the day consisted of having a sandwich for her main meal, if she was lucky. She glanced down at the way her clothes were now hanging on her. When she'd arrived, almost two years earlier, she'd been at least a stone, if not more, heavier.

Once April and Willow had eaten, Jacinda played with them again for another hour before she bathed and put them to bed. The children loved their bath time; they were at their happiest splashing about in the water, playfully squirting each other. Jacinda knew there would be a lot of cleaning up to do. However, it would be worth watching the utter joy on their faces.

"Come on, you two, it's time to get out now."

After the usual round of complaints, April and Willow finally relented. She dried them, dressed them in their pyjamas and opened the bathroom door. Standing in the hallway were Mr and Mrs Knox, smiling at the children.

"Have fun, did you?" Mrs Knox asked.

"We did, Mummy. I'm tired now," April replied sleepily, the warmth of the bath apparently doing what it was supposed to do.

Jacinda tucked April and Willow into their beds under the watchful gaze of the parents and then left the room. No need for her to read them a bedtime story tonight as their eyelids were already drooping.

She closed the door to the bedroom the children shared.

Mrs Knox took two paces towards her. She prodded Jacinda in the chest. "Have your meal then get out of our sight. We don't want to see or hear from you until the morning, got that?"

Jacinda nodded. That suited her. She ran down the stairs and into the kitchen, her tummy rumbling expectantly. She lifted the cover on the plate of food, and her heart sank. One sprig of broccoli and a few slithers of cheese. *And I'm supposed to survive and look after their sprogs on that?* She strained her neck, listening for movement. There was none. She tiptoed across the kitchen floor to the bread bin and removed a slice of wholemeal bread, hoping that would add a few of the calories the meal was lacking. She'd nearly made it back to her seat when the door burst open and Mr Knox came storming into the room. His grinning wife lingered in the doorway, her arms folded.

Shit!

Jacinda was in trouble. How much trouble remained to be seen. "I'm sorry. I was hungry. Please, please forgive me."

Mr Knox's response came swiftly, in the form of a punch to the stomach. "I'd better make sure your hunger pangs disperse quickly then. Has that done the trick?" he asked, letting out a demented laugh.

Jacinda wished she could curl up and die, she'd had enough. Enough of this bullying, this abusive behaviour. The torments they threw at her every day. The sleepless nights she'd endured. She was bone tired and ready to give up; however, God refused to take her or step in and help her come to that. If there was a god up there and He was looking down on her but didn't intervene, what did that tell her? That He approved of the way they treated her?

"Yes, thank you. I'll go to my room now."

She walked towards the door. Mrs Knox narrowed her gaze during her approach. Jacinda paused. The woman continued to block the doorway, her arms still folded in an obstinate stance.

"Please, can I get past, Mrs Knox?" she whispered.

Mrs Knox did the unthinkable—spat in her face and then stepped to one side. Jacinda ran past the hateful woman, up to her room. She closed her bedroom door, her stomach aching from the blow she'd received which overshadowed the feeling of hunger she'd had previously. She crossed the room to her bed, placed the pillow in front of her and cried silent tears in case they heard her.

I have to get out of here. Sooner rather than later. This week! Tonight would be perfect. But how? The Knoxes always ensure the house is secured well at night.

She glanced over at her window. Although her bedroom was on the second floor, below her stood the garage. She'd often pondered her escape route in the past but she'd been too much of a coward to consider it. Now, she was desperate. She tried to block out what the consequences of such a dangerous mission would be. To her, her life was no longer worth living. Crossing the floor, avoiding the floorboards she knew creaked, she peered out of the window. From an early age she'd been scared of heights. The question was: would she be able to overcome her fears to escape this nightmare? She nodded. Yes, she would need to delve deep into her resolve to pluck up the courage to do it.

She was determined that tonight would be when she'd execute her audacious plan.

2

She lay there listening, waiting for the time to come. She could hear movement in the room next door, the master bedroom. It was obvious the couple were having sex. Every night was the same. She heard them at it, like rabbits most nights. Had the children not been around, she suspected the whole street would have heard the sex games they participated in nightly. She hated listening to them, it was a constant reminder of what he did to her, to punish her.

In the dead of the night, at two-fifteen, Jacinda left her bed. She dressed in the clean clothes she'd laid out for her adventure and packed the rest of her clothes in the suitcase. She hadn't quite worked out how she was going to get that out of the window yet—she considered that to be the least of her worries at this point. Her own safety had to be the utmost consideration in her plan, not her belongings.

She hunted at the bottom of her wardrobe and found a couple of belts which had slipped off the hangers. After tying them together, she measured the length—only five feet, but it would have to do. With everything she owned, which wasn't much, now in the case and the holdall, she inched open the window. Luckily it was the older, sash type, which would enable her to squeeze her case and herself through without much effort. Her heart pounded violently; her breath became erratic with every step she took now. *I can't do it! What if I fall and break my neck? It'll be better than continuing to work here. Do it! I have to.* Her inner voices argued with each other.

After lowering her bag onto the pitch roof of the garage, she let it go. It clattered and tumbled into the shrubs to the side. She paused and listened, making sure she hadn't disturbed the couple next door. Moments later, she took the plunge and emerged through the window. She gasped for breath and sat on the sill to compose herself and her thoughts. *It's only a short drop, I'll be fine. I have no other option open to me...not if I want to live.*

Teetering on the edge of the sill, she threw her holdall and flinched as it hit the ground with a loud thud. *This is it...I have to go now, there's no turning back.* She rotated, gripped tightly the sill and lowered herself down the side of the house. The garage roof was four feet below her. The fear took her breath away. Her erratic heartbeat was almost too much, and she became light-headed. She pushed through the barriers of the emotions welling up inside as her parents' smiling faces entered her mind. *If nothing else, I'll do it for them. I miss them so much.*

She sucked in a final steadying breath and committed. She launched herself and landed on her knees. The pain was excruciating. She resisted the urge to cry out and peered down to see where she could land without further injuring herself. Wincing, she scrambled across the roof to the other end where she remembered a thick hedge was located. After testing it would hold her weight, she lowered herself onto the top. She released her grip on the edge of the tiles and ended up sinking into the middle of the privet.

Her knee was swelling up; it was already tight against her jeans. All she had to do now was leave the garden and try to flag down a taxi. It was then that realisation struck. She had no money, not even for a simple taxi or bus fare. She wrestled with the branches and the odd thorny bramble intent on leaving their mark on her already battered and bruised body. Finally, she found the energy and the coordination to right herself and leave the confines of the hedge. Collecting her bag and suitcase, she took one look back at the house and spotted a figure standing at the window. It was *her*. Mrs Knox was staring at her, giving her one of her evil smiles.

Jacinda was mortified. She had to run as fast as she could now, but how was she supposed to do that with a bum knee? She turned and yelped as she struck something solid in her path. It was Mr Knox. Her heart raced faster; Jacinda feared she was going to have a heart attack any second.

"Where the fuck do you think you're going?" he demanded, his face lowering to within inches of her own.

"Please, please let me go. I want to go home. I need to go home. To see my parents."

"Why? To tell them?"

"No. I would never tell anyone…I swear. You have to believe me."

"Do I?" He grasped her around the throat. "Don't tell me what I have to do, you hear me? You're a nobody. The lowest of the low." He swivelled her in place and steered her towards the front door of the house.

Mrs Knox was standing there, waiting for them.

Jacinda, still holding her holdall and the suitcase, her knee giving her gyp, walked slowly. He pushed her in the back, low down near her kidneys. She had to force herself to remain upright. Tears threatened to fall. She could only imagine what lay ahead of her now, after being discovered trying to escape. Her hands shook—she had no way of stopping her body reacting to the fear running through her veins.

In the hallway, Mr Knox finally removed the suitcase from her hand. He strode over to the door beneath the stairs and opened it. Her heart sank…the basement.

"Please, don't put me in there." Her plea was barely audible.

He pointed at the dark space then leaned over and switched on the light. "Down there, now. Make a single noise, and I'll kill you."

Jacinda gulped and nodded. Every step she took was mind-numbingly more painful than the last. Her pain escalated to another level altogether when she began her descent into the cold basement. She'd only been down here once before, but it was enough to make her never want to visit the cobweb-ridden, damp confines again. Tears blurred her vision. Something in her gut made her fear this visit even more than the last. On that occasion, she was tortured by the couple after Willow had ripped his trousers at the park on one of the slides, as if that was her fault.

Two sets of footsteps followed her down the rickety stairs. At the bottom, wincing, she stood to one side and waited for the couple to join her. Her gaze transfixed on the locked door in the corner that she knew awaited her. Mr Knox yanked her by the arm and pulled her the four feet towards the door. The cobwebs in all the corners were far thicker than when she'd been holed up down here. She shuddered at the thought of the eight-legged creatures scurrying across her skin and through her long brown hair. That alone would have been torture enough; however, she was more than aware of what went on in the mind of her two capturers. The wicked thoughts that ran through their minds. The ice that flowed through their cores.

By the time they had finished with her, she knew her life would be hanging by a thread.

She silently uttered a prayer, pleading for His help, aware that He'd probably look the other way, just like He had the many times the couple had punished her over the past two years.

"Please, don't do this. I swear I'll never try to leave again."

Mr Knox shook his head slowly. "You won't get the chance. Get in there. You'll stay there until we decide what to do with you. I'm warning you now, it won't be pretty. You've really angered us this time. Your punishment will be far worse than you've ever experienced before. We will not tolerate such behaviour from our staff. We give you everything you need. Feed you, give you a comfortable bed to sleep in, and this is how you repay us, by trying to escape. The children love you. How could you even think about running out on them at a time when they need you most in their lives? How dare you? You selfish bitch."

Jacinda didn't have it in her to say anything in her defence, there was no point. Once Mr Knox's mind was made up, there was no shifting him.

"What do you have to say for yourself?"

"Nothing, except I was wrong. If you could find it in your hearts to forgive me, to even consider giving me a week's holiday so that I could travel to Scotland to see my folks…" She hadn't had a holiday since she'd arrived. She realised the likelihood of obtaining one now that they'd uncovered her plan to escape was non-existent.

"Nope, not going to happen. You think what you tried to do tonight warrants us treating you well? You've shown how much you respect us by trying to abscond. We welcomed you as part of our family, and this is the gratitude you show us in return. No, you'll remain down here until we see fit to welcome you into our home again. The children will be told that you have gone away for a few days' rest."

Jacinda's mouth dropped open.

Mr Knox's speech wasn't finished yet. Taking another pace forward, he lowered his head until their lips were inches apart. He sneered. "If we hear one blasted word from you, I'll travel to Scotland and slit your parents' throats."

"No. Please. Don't hurt them."

He stepped back. "Don't force me to carry out my threat, you hear me?"

She swallowed down the acid burning her throat. "Please, I understand. I'm so sorry. Won't you forgive me? Forgive my sins?"

"It will take a lot more than your simplistic words for that to happen. Spend a few days down here alone, and we'll reassess the situation."

She nodded. He pushed her into the room which would become her cell for the next few days. The door slammed, the noise echoing in her surroundings. She wrapped her arms around herself, trying to ward off the chill already seeping into her bones. She had no idea if she was going to survive the next forty-eight hours, or however long they decided to leave her down here without food or water.

They were evil, pure and simple, and her life was going to get a whole lot worse because of her foolish attempt to escape.

3

Jacinda woke with a stiff neck and excruciating pain in her swollen knee. Tears spilled onto her cheeks as she realised she'd recently wet herself. Now her legs stung, adding to her discomfort. She had no way of knowing what time of day it was. She'd never been one for wearing a watch, and there were no windows in her cell.

A noise in the basement drew her attention. She wrapped her arms around her legs and waited with bated breath for the door to open. The key turned, and the door sprang open. Standing in the opening was Mr Knox, a sneer on his smug face. "You're awake then."

"Yes. I'm sorry," she muttered, hoping her apology would be sufficient and he'd take pity on her and let her at least tend to her duties once more. She missed April and Willow.

"Are you? How sorry?" He took a few steps forward.

She retreated, shuffling backwards into the corner she'd spent most of the night avoiding because of the thickness of the web. Jacinda placed a hand over her mouth to stop herself from screaming when a large, thick-legged spider ran over her hair and down her face. Shuddering, she stared up at her boss. "Please don't hurt me. I've been punished enough."

He laughed, raucously at first and then toned it down a little, she presumed so the other residents in the house didn't hear him. *Are the kids still at home? What would happen if I cried out for help? Would they come down here to see me?* It was dumb of her to think like that. Knox had already warned her what would happen if she attempted to do that. She could take all the punishment they meted out, but what she couldn't accept was if he carried out his threat and went to Scotland to hurt her parents.

"Enough? Is that what you truly think? After trying to escape like that? You clearly have no idea about the magnitude of what you've done. You tried to desert our children, the same children who idolise you. Who worship you, Lord knows why that is. You're a worthless piece of shit. An ungrateful individual who attempted to run away from the perfect job. We treat you well, don't we?" He took another couple of steps into the cell.

"Yes. I'm sorry. I was desperate to see my parents. I need a holiday. I haven't had one for two years."

He leaned down and got in her face, his spittle flying and slapping on her cheeks. "*We* tell you when you can leave this house. April and Willow need you to care for them. Mrs Knox and I are exceptionally busy people. We pay you to care for our children because we simply don't have the time to do that ourselves. And this is how you repay us…by running out on us?"

He was delusional. They paid her a pittance to live on so that she could buy the bare necessities such as toothpaste, deodorant, shampoo and sanitary towels. Nothing more for any possible treats such as chocolate or a sandwich she could stash in her room for when hunger struck.

"I'm sorry," she muttered, playing along with him for now, not knowing what else she could do, given the pain she was in.

"Are you? How sorry?"

Is he asking a trick question? "I don't understand," she eventually said.

"The children asked after you this morning. We told them you'd gone away for a few days. That way, they won't be expecting you to be around and it will give you the opportunity to contemplate just how sorry you are. And, of course, to show me personally how desperate you are to make amends."

She couldn't believe what she was hearing. She was aware that she'd pissed herself. He must have realised that, smelt it even, and yet he was here telling her what he expected from her when all she wanted to do was have a long luxurious soak in a bath to cleanse the filth from her and to bathe her aching knee. "Please, I'll do anything you want, but not here."

"You think I need your permission to take what I want?" He laughed again and struck her across the face, hard enough to snap her head to the side.

She struggled in her attempt not to cry out. Tempted beyond words, the only thing preventing her was his threat lingering in her head.

Suddenly he retreated out of the room. "You'll wait. I have an important conference call to make. All I wanted to do was come down here and brighten my day, and yours, of course. Enjoy the peace and quiet. Oh, and the new friendships you've made with your creepy cellmates. If you're good, next time I might even bring you a drink and something to eat. Until then, I wouldn't contemplate wasting that piss of yours. I hear it's supposed to be good for the body."

The door slammed. Alone and in the dark again, she buried her head in her hands and sobbed. *What have I done to deserve this? I've never wronged anyone in my life. Always accepted that I have to work hard in this world for little in return. Clearly that was never enough. And now this! How the hell am I going to get out of this situation? Will I ever get out of it? What if their intention is to keep me here until they've had enough of me and then decide to end my miserable life? Will I find that a blessed relief?* She thought over the final question she'd asked herself and nodded—yes, she thought she would. A relief to never again feel fear running through her veins.

Jacinda wrapped her arms around her knees and rocked back and forth, wincing now and again at the pain emanating from her poorly knee. It was clear she needed hospital treatment, but there was no way of her getting that. Eventually, she drifted off to sleep again, only to be awoken by Mr Knox entering the room several hours later. The dull basement light behind him highlighted a can of Coke and a sandwich in his right hand.

"You want them?"

She reached for the items. "Please, I'm starving."

He shook his head. "You don't know the meaning of the word. Starving is when you're skin and bones, just like the little children in Africa."

"I apologise, I was wrong to say that. I'm peckish," she corrected herself, hoping to dampen down the anger she saw in his eyes.

"That's better. Remember, there are always people worse off than you in this world."

"I'll be sure to think about that in the future."

He relented and gave her the food and drink. She resisted the temptation to snatch them out of his grasp, in case he changed his mind and closed the door again, taking the goodies with him. He smiled down at her and nodded, encouraging her to eat.

He leaned against the rotten doorframe and watched her nibble on her sandwich and wash each mouthful down with the fizzy Coke. The bubbles travelled down her oesophagus and into her empty stomach. The sensation was a weird one and like nothing she'd ever experienced before. Still, she was grateful for the treats he'd provided, no matter how meagre. After all this time on rationed food, she doubted whether she'd be able to face a full meal again in the future.

"Satisfied now, are you?"

She nodded, unsure which way the conversation would go next.

"Good. Now you can show me how appreciative you are. Strip off."

Jacinda closed her eyes. *How could he even consider raping me when I'm in dire need of a shower?*

She might have thought that; however, she stripped off nevertheless. He roughly placed her against the wall and pounded her from behind. Again, she was both relieved and grateful that his stamina wasn't up to scratch.

"Get dressed. You disgust me."

Obviously not enough, otherwise you wouldn't continue to rape me, you bastard.

After getting dressed, he left the room. She found herself alone again and in the dark with only her thoughts and the spiders to keep her company.

Blocking out what he'd done to her, she started daydreaming. She reminisced about her wonderful childhood, the time when her parents doted on her. Treated her like a goddess. Made sure she didn't want for anything. How she had missed them both. The number of nights she'd lain awake, silently pleading with them to come and get her. Her parents were busy people, though. Wrapped up in their own printing business—being self-employed sucked. No one ever had the time to think of those around them, too busy trying to grow the business, often intent on making ends meet.

Had it really been two years since either of her parents had held her in their arms? Would she ever share that type of contact with her parents in the future? She doubted it. Over the years, the Knoxes had given her permission to contact her parents via the house phone, providing they were there listening in on the conversation. That way, they ensured she kept her tone light and breezy, making sure her parents hadn't cottoned on to the trauma the couple were putting her through.

In the past, she had persuaded her parents that she was happy and settled in Manchester and that she was enjoying her role too much to head north to see them. Being super-busy people, they had appreciated what she was saying. That had pained her, to think her parents were prepared to give up on her like that. She knew it wasn't intentional and that their prime goal in life was to create a successful business. Once they had started down that route, it was proving impossible to get back to their normal lives and give their only daughter the attention she deserved.

She was being harsh on them. All parents had the right to live their lives how they saw fit once their children flew the nest. Picturing her mother's beautiful face and the concern wrinkled into her father's brow, she felt guilty for slating them for their lack of interest in her.

With nothing else for her to do, Jacinda drifted off again. The lock turning in the door startled her from a dream in which she was sleeping in her own bed back in Scotland, her mother running around after her, tending to her every need.

She leapt to her feet and went towards the light. The door was open, and yet neither Mr nor Mrs Knox was anywhere to be seen. *What's going on? Is this the end of my punishment? Am I free to go now? To care for the children once more?* She tentatively placed one foot over the threshold and peered around the open door. The couple stood behind it, sniggering like teenagers. She stared at them, uncertain what to say or do next.

The door swung back and hit her. She grunted and stumbled backwards, hobbling because of her knee.

Mr Knox latched on to her arm, preventing her from hitting the floor. His wife stood in front of her. She had something in her hand—a roll of duct tape.

"No, please. Anything but that."

The couple laughed. It echoed around the basement; it was enough to send an icy shiver scampering down her spine.

While Mr Knox held her arms behind her, Mrs Knox tore off a strip of tape and stuck it over Jacinda's mouth. She tried hard to make it difficult for Mrs Knox, but she stamped on Jacinda's feet to keep her still.

Her eyes widened when Mrs Knox withdrew a large kitchen knife and slashed it through Jacinda's clothes. *What the hell is she doing? This can't be happening. Is this the end?*

Mr and Mrs Knox's gazes locked. They appeared caught up in their own fantasy to realise what was going on, the damage they were carrying out.

Jacinda's fear escalated. She fought hard to release herself from Mr Knox's grip. The lashes doubled in frequency, cutting deeper into her flesh now. The couple kissed. *Are they getting off on this? Is this a fetish of theirs? To kill someone in order to get aroused?* No matter what questions filled her mind, the reality was that Jacinda's life hung in the balance. Her legs weakened due to the amount of blood she had lost, and still the couple's lips were locked, the slashes with the blade never-ending.

If there is a god up there, take me now. I've had it with this world. Show me what happiness there is to be had on the other side, please.

Mr Knox let go of her arms, and she tumbled to the floor. The couple continued to kiss, groaning with desire while Jacinda groaned in agony.

"No, stop. Let's save this for after," Mr Knox said, tracing a loving finger down his wife's cheek.

Mrs Knox stared down at Jacinda. "Yes, I've had it with her. She's ticked me off once too often. She has never cared properly for Willow and April. Let's finish her off and get someone new."

Mr Knox nodded in acquiescence, then they turned their full attention on Jacinda. She cowered from the blows raining down on her until everything went black.

~

"Is she dead?" Sadie asked.

"Seems that way. I never wanted her to die. I only ever wanted to punish her," Leonard replied.

"Is that you saying that or your dick?"

He chuckled. "You know me so well."

Sadie shrugged. "What next? How are we going to dispose of this one?"

"Let's face it, she's not going anywhere. That gives us enough time to pack up the house and get out of here."

"Not again? I'm not sure how long I can keep doing this, Leonard. Maybe we should settle down and start enjoying life more. The children can do without this disruption at school."

"You should have thought about that before you began slashing at her. You're the one who finished her off."

Sadie stood back and crossed her arms. "How dare you say that? This was a joint effort. She'd outlived her usefulness, we both agreed on that, didn't we?"

"There's no point in us discussing this further, what's done is done. We need to work quickly now, get away from here within the next few days. She has friends, other nannies in the area. We don't want to arouse their suspicions."

Sadie laughed. "She never had any friends. Not people who cared about what she got up to anyway."

"Whatever. I'm not going to argue the toss with you about that now. We have work to do. We need to relocate and quickly."

"Where? Do we stick another pin in the map and see where that leads us?"

"No, this time we need to think things through properly. There's our work to consider. We're making good money now, it would be a shame to let that side of things slide."

"How can we continue to trade? We'll need to create different identities all over again, for fuck's sake."

"I'm warning you, Sadie, don't go pulling one of your foul moods on me. You're the one responsible for ending her life. You were too eager. I wanted to punish her some more, keep her down here for a few more days, to give me some thinking time, but would you listen? No. Take the bull by the horns and dive straight in, that's you all over."

"Whatever. There's no point going round and round in circles. We have to get our shit together and swiftly. I repeat, what are we going to do with the body?"

He tapped the side of his nose and leaned in for a kiss. "Leave that to me. Now get upstairs and show me how much you love me."

He chased the screaming Sadie up the two flights of stairs and into the bedroom, his mind on one thing only—satisfying his needs.

4

*H*ero heaved out a weary sigh. He threw an arm around his wife's shoulders and pulled her close. "It's nice to have an early night for a change."

Fay placed a hand on his chest and swirled her forefinger in his hairs, the way she always did. "I'm glad the kids behaved tonight and went to bed without any hassle after their bath. I swear those girls are getting naughtier with each passing year."

"Don't say that. They're six now, what the heck are they going to be like when they're eighteen?"

Fay glanced at him and rolled her eyes. "I don't even want to think about that. Maybe Louie will help us out there."

Hero frowned. "Are you saying what I think you're saying? You're hoping he'll spy on them and report back to us?"

Fay pushed away from his chest and sat up. "Wow, I wasn't thinking anything of the sort. However, now you've mentioned it…"

He leaned over and kissed her. "He'll do anything we ask him to where the twins are concerned. He adores them."

Fay settled down in position again. "Family is everything to him. He loves those girls. It doesn't matter that there's an age gap of five years. He doesn't seem to care. Maybe that'll change now he's started secondary school."

"I can't see it. He's a level-headed lad. Add smart and compassionate to the list, and that just about sums him up perfectly."

"I know we might complain about them running us ragged at times, but listening to some of the horrific tales some of the mothers at the school gate describe, our three are angels." Fay held her crossed fingers in the air.

Hero did the same. It didn't prevent memories of a recent encounter he'd had with a group of teenagers running through his mind, however. There were six of them, varying ages from eleven up to fifteen. They'd been causing havoc in the town for around a month. The eldest boy's father had been sent to prison, and the boy was in the throes of rebelling against society. Vandalising cars at night, buying and drinking alcohol on street corners. It was the boy's own mother who had dobbed him in to the police, fearful of him ending up like his father, behind bars. Hero had interviewed the lads, torn into them at the station, with their parents' permission.

Thankfully, the boys had done the right thing and mended their ways, at least for now.

Hero was feeling nice and relaxed after a few stressful days of long shifts. He was in the process of drifting off to sleep, but his mobile vibrating on the bedside table disrupted his zen-like state. "Damn, it's probably Mum. I said I'd ring her tonight and I forgot."

"You'd better answer it then, she'll be worried about you."

He retrieved his mobile and tutted once he'd spotted the caller ID. "It's work, not Mum. I should have ignored it."

Fay chuckled and sat up again. "The likelihood of you doing that is non-existent, and you know it."

"You know me far too well. Here goes." He answered the call. "DI Hero Nelson."

"I'm sorry to disturb your evening, sir, but you're needed at a crime scene."

"Can't someone else handle it?"

"Everyone else is busy tonight, sir. I can get them to report to the scene once they're free…"

"Why do I sense a *but* coming here?" he asked the female on control.

"It's a nasty one, sir. It has your name written all over it."

If he wasn't so ticked off by the disruption, he would have laughed. "Okay, you've ground me down. What are the details?" He threw the covers back and slipped out of bed.

Fay leapt out and gathered his clothes for him, placing clean underwear on top of the pile while he jotted down the address.

"I'll be there in a maximum of fifteen. Do me a favour and ring my partner. If I'm getting called out then so is she."

"My colleague has already actioned that, sir. She's en route now."

"Good." He hung up and dashed into the bathroom for a quick wash and squeezed out a wee. There was no telling when the opportunity would arise to have another one in the coming hours.

Entering the bedroom, he found Fay back in bed and longed to be beside her. "Sorry, love. So much for our once-in-a-blue-moon early night, eh?"

"There'll be plenty of others. Stay safe out there."

Once he was dressed, he kissed her on the lips. "I love you, Mrs Nelson."

He snatched up his notebook and rushed out of the house. The air was blue in the car, his temper building rapidly as he drove through the darkness to the address out in Cheadle Hulme. A car pulled out of a side road in front of him. He blasted the horn, and the driver gave him the finger. Had he not been in a rush, he would have pulled the guy over and given him a firm warning. As it was, he switched on his police light and sped past the man's car. His face was a picture.

"You won't do that again in a hurry, will you, tosser?"

Ten minutes later, Hero drew up outside a detached house in a quiet cul-de-sac. Julie's car was already on site. He collected his paper suit from the boot of his car and approached the house. The uniformed officer on duty at the front door smiled and let him into the house.

"Shaw, are you in here?"

"In the kitchen, guv."

Hero slipped his suit on, placed the blue covers over his footwear and went in search of his partner. The house appeared to be in good condition from what he could tell from the hallway, but it looked a little too bare and modernistic for his liking, not homely in the slightest. It wasn't until he reached the kitchen, which was devoid of any furniture, that he realised the house wasn't lived in.

"What have we got, Julie?"

"Evening, sir. A bit of an odd one. The house is empty as you can see, and yet someone lit a barbecue in the back garden."

"Squatters? Vagrants? What are you saying?"

"That's just it, sir, I'm not sure what I'm saying. All I know is that the fire was raging enough to concern the neighbours. A few of them reported it at the same time. When the fire brigade showed up, this is what they found."

"Do you have to be so cryptic? Can't you tell me the facts right away for a change?" he snapped, cringing at the tone he'd used. "Sorry, I'm tired and irritable. Ignore me."

"Aren't we all, sir? Come with me." She marched past him, clipping his shoulder intentionally, and raced into the garden where five firemen were standing around. Some of them were speaking to uniformed officers while the others shuffled their feet. "Statements. I told them to get their statements down before they rushed off."

"Good idea. Come on, Julie, let me in on the secret?"

"This way, sir." She trudged across the longish grass towards the smoking barbecue and pointed. "There. That's what they found."

Hero stopped next to her, studied the blackened equipment for a second or two and turned back to face her. "You've got me. So, someone had a barbecue. The last time I heard that wasn't against the law."

Shaw inhaled a large breath which expanded her chest. Hero knew this movement well—his partner was trying hard to suppress her annoyance.

"There's a body burning in the barbecue, sir."

"Shit! Really?" He took a few steps closer and covered his mouth and nose. The smell was just like a hog roast he'd been invited to at his friend's house. *Shit, who knew burning flesh could smell like that? No wonder there are cannibals in this world.*

"Yep. Horrendous, right? Who would do such a thing?"

He retreated a few steps, far enough back so he could no longer smell the remains. "Who spotted it?"

Shaw pointed across the lawn to one of the firemen who was giving his statement. "Todd Johnson, sir. He saw a bone and felt something wasn't right and called it in."

"Good man. Okay, where are SOCO and the pathologist? We need them here, ASAP."

"I've tried chasing them up, but they're caught up at another scene, a traffic accident on the M6."

"Damn. Okay." He glanced skywards. "I swear it's going to piss down soon. We need to get this scene covered, just in case."

"That's going to be hard to do if it's still smouldering, surely?"

"Let me ring Gerrard, see how long he's going to be and see what he recommends we do to preserve the scene."

Julie nodded and walked back into the house. Hero kicked out at a clump of grass while he waited for Gerrard to answer the call.

"What is it?"

"Nice greeting. Hello to you, too."

"I knew it was you. I told your sidekick what's on my agenda. I don't appreciate being hounded every ten minutes or so, Nelson."

"Bloody hell! You might want to tone down that anger of yours, mate, before you burst a blood vessel. Okay, hear me out. I'm at the scene. In case you hadn't noticed, it looks like it's going to tip down any minute. I'm concerned about the scene and was ringing up to see if you've got any suggestions on how we can shield it from the elements. The thing is, I thought about placing a sheet over it, but the darn thing is still smouldering. Do you want me to sanction the firemen to carry on or what? I don't have enough experience of burning bodies to call the shots."

"Sarcastic as ever. No, let it die down naturally. I'll make a call, get a technician out of his bed just for you to preserve the scene."

"Now who's being sarcastic? Right, I'll leave you to get on with things there and see you, when?"

"I'm going to be at least another thirty minutes here. It ain't pretty. They're just clearing up the road and opening it now. Three vehicles, one concertinaed with two pensioners dead inside."

"That's tough. Sorry for being such a grouch, mate. You get on. Place the call for me."

"Organising that now. See you soon—if you're still there and not back in bed by the time I get there."

"I'll be here for the duration." Hero ended the call, his thoughts drifting for a moment to his father whom he'd lost two years previously. Tears misted his eyes. He turned his back to face the brick wall behind him and wiped the sleeve of his jacket across his eyes.

"Are you all right, sir?"

Damn! Why does Shaw always have to show up when I'm in a contemplative mood?

"I'm fine. I think the smoke got in my eyes a little. Gerrard is sending a technician over. I'm presuming he'll erect a marquee when he gets here. Until then, we need to pray the rain holds off."

"Rightio. Is there anything else you want me to do?"

"Help get the statements, so these busy men can get back on duty. Have you thought about that?"

"I was about to suggest the same. There's no need for you to keep sniping at me. I wasn't the one who rang you, getting you out of your warm, cosy bed."

"Sorry. I didn't mean to have a pop. We'll take down the statements between us. If nothing else, it'll help pass the time until Gerrard and his crew get here."

"Sounds like a plan. I'll fetch a few forms from the car. I made some enquiries, and there are only two more statements to obtain, one each."

"Good stuff."

Julie disappeared into the house and returned carrying the forms. She handed one to him, and they approached the group of firemen.

"Are we going to be held up for long, boss?" the eldest of the three said.

"We're trying to alleviate that for you. Who hasn't made a statement yet?"

"Steve and Colin."

"Steve, why don't you go with my partner, Julie, here? And Colin, you can come with me. We'll go inside where it's warmer, gents."

The two men nodded and walked into the house with Hero and Julie. She stood in one corner of the vast kitchen, taking down Steve's statement while Hero spoke to Colin.

"Can you go through what happened when you arrived at the scene?"

"Sure. Want me to say it slowly?" Colin asked, a twinkle in his eye.

"If you wouldn't mind? My shorthand isn't up to scratch these days."

Colin sniggered. "I know what you mean. Right, we received the call to attend the blaze. We got here around twenty minutes later. The fire was still going strong. A couple of us started dousing it when Todd shouted that he'd spotted something. We stopped to take a closer look and saw what appeared to be a human femur. A few of us were sick near the scene, sorry about that. It was all too much for the guys. Not the type of thing you expect to find when putting out a bloody barbie, is it? Jesus, who'd sink to that level, eh?"

Hero sighed heavily. "That's what we're going to have to figure out. The house seems empty, no residents on site, which is only going to make our job harder."

"Done a moonlight flit, you reckon?"

"So it would appear. Getting back to what happened next," Hero urged, not keen on speculating a crime with anyone other than his team.

"Sorry, I'm prone to asking a lot of questions myself. It was a toss-up whether I joined the force or the brigade. Obviously I chose the latter, although after discovering something like this and the investigation side of things you guys are going to have to delve into...well, there are days when I regret that decision."

"Go with your heart. You're young enough. We're always on the lookout for new recruits. The job is getting tougher these days, though. It's no longer perceived as an easy ride to those within the force."

"Nothing like telling someone how it is in the hope of putting them off, hey, man?"

"Sorry, that definitely wasn't my intention. Don't tell me your job is a piece of cake nowadays either?"

"It is mostly, money for old rope most of the time, except when we stumble upon something like this. Gruesome ain't the word, is it? Damn, some days I wish I'd stayed in bed. This is one of those days."

"Me, too. I'd just climbed into mine, promised the missus we'd get the kids out of the way and have an early night ourselves. That went to pot when the blasted call came in. Probably won't get to bed tonight now, knowing how cases like this ruddy pan out."

"Jesus, do you get many bodies found in a barbie, then?"

"No, this is a first for me. So, after Todd put a halt to things, what happened next?"

"Well, the boss rang your lot. It's awful, ain't it? I'd prefer to extinguish the flames completely, but the boss instructed us to leave well alone. He's experienced enough to know how damaging water can be to a crime scene. Have you smelt it?" He retched. "Not sure I'll ever cook pork again after smelling that shit. Sorry, that was disrespectful to the victim."

Hero nodded. "It was. You know what? I thought the same bloody thing. Is that it?"

"Yep, that's about it, we called a halt to the proceedings and waited for your lot to show up."

"Thanks. Thinking back to when you arrived at the scene, did you notice anyone outside the house at all?"

"No, nothing as far as I can remember. We came in through the side gate. It was locked—one of the guys had to give Todd a leg up to unlock it from this side. The more I think about it, the more shocked I am. Why would a person do that, kill someone? I'm not jumping the gun there, am I? And then burn the body in the barbie and take off like that? I can't work it out meself."

"Again, that's something we're going to have to figure out."

"Another thing I thought about, not sure if it'll be useful to you or not."

"Go on, I'm all ears," Hero prompted.

Colin lowered his voice so the others couldn't hear. "Whoever did it must have cut up the body first, wouldn't you say?"

Hero nodded. "I was thinking along the same lines, although I'd rather leave that up to the pathologist to confirm. Ghastly thought nonetheless."

Colin glanced over his shoulder and leaned in close. "One of my relatives used to live around here. Not sure if you're aware of this, but these houses have cellars."

Hero widened his eyes. "I wasn't aware of that. Thanks for the info. I'll take a look after we've finished your statement."

"Glad to be of help. My take is that the body was probably cut up down there and then they tried to get rid of it on the grill."

Hero cringed. "Sounds like a plausible theory. Either you have a copper's brain or you read a lot of crime novels."

"The former. Hey, this has really got my juices going. After speaking to you, I mean. Maybe I'll take your advice and apply after all."

There was another option Hero didn't voice: *This man could very well be the killer.* He shook his head, ridding himself of such a ludicrous thought.

With the statement of events completed, Hero dismissed Colin and joined Julie, who was also adding the finishing touches to her statement with Steve.

"Thanks for this. You're free to go now." Julie smiled briefly at the man.

"Ring me if you need anything else." Steve grinned and rejoined his team.

Hero nudged his partner and whispered, "Looks like someone has taken a shine to you."

Julie shuddered and flashed the wedding ring on her finger at him.

"I couldn't give a monkey's arse, I'm spoken for. Rob and I are very happy together."

Hero shrugged. "I was winding you up, Shaw. It's about time you figured out when I'm pulling your leg and when I'm being serious."

Julie's cheeks coloured up. "Whatever."

Hero chuckled. "The chap I was speaking to, a wannabe copper, came up with a suggestion I think we should check out while we're waiting for Gerrard to arrive."

"What's that?"

"Come with me, you'll soon find out."

Julie followed Hero through the house. He searched the hallway, pulling open several doors before he found the likely one he was searching for. "Ah-ha...here it is."

Julie peered around him. "A cellar?"

"Indeed. Be careful on your way down."

"I can't." Julie backed up and pinned herself against the wall in the hallway.

"There's no such word as *can't*, especially if you're a copper. Get a grip, woman."

She shook her head, her face draining of its usual colour. "No way. You're on your own on this one, guv. Sack me if you want, there's no way I'm going down there."

Hero grunted and continued on his journey, his steps tentative at first until his eyes grew accustomed to the dark confines. The light above his head sprang to life.

"Is that better?" Julie shouted from the doorway.

"Much, thank you. You should come down here...no, on second thoughts, scrub that...Jesus...what the hell?"

Once the energy-saving bulb reached its maximum intensity, the gruesome sight in front of him had him shaking his head. He gagged a few times but just about managed to hang on to the Chinese takeaway he'd treated the family to that evening. There was blood everywhere. If he'd taken a step farther...well, the pathologist would have had his knackers between two slices of bread.

"What is it?" Julie shouted.

"Get down here and see for yourself."

"I can't. The fear is too much. I'm sorry."

"Shaw, come halfway. You need to see this."

The stairs creaked a little. "Jesus…seriously? Oh God, I think I'm going to puke." She ran back up the stairs.

If Hero hadn't been in a state of shock he would have creased up with laughter. Instead, he decided to retreat and leave.

Julie's colour was even paler than when he'd stepped foot in the cellar. "Are you all right?"

"Nothing ten cups of coffee wouldn't put right."

"Hello, hello…what's going on here then?" Gerrard's booming voice almost catapulted Hero through the ceiling to the bedroom above.

"What the heck…you scared the crap out of me. It's about time you showed up."

"Thanks, it's nice to see you, too. Why are you two looking so glum?"

Hero pointed to the open doorway. "You'll soon find out."

"Sounds ominous. You want to show me or shall I see for myself?"

"I'd rather not."

Gerrard rolled his eyes and shook his head. Moments later, once he'd reached the bottom of the stairs, a few choice expletives came their way.

"Get SOCO down here. No, wait, I'm coming up. I need to see the body first, this can wait."

Gerrard resurfaced and exhaled a large breath. "Despicable that a person could do that to another human being."

"You read my mind. Here, let me show you the way."

The three of them exited the house and crossed the lawn to the barbecue. "As if what was in the cellar wasn't enough. Still, after all that blood loss, I'm not surprised to find there are body parts on site. Inventive way of getting rid of a corpse, wouldn't you agree?"

Hero couldn't believe what he was hearing. "Not really. Quite dumb in my book."

Gerrard tilted his head and frowned. "How so?"

"Because they alerted the neighbours, who in turn, rang the fire brigade, who then rang us once they arrived and realised what they were dealing with."

"Ah yes, of course. Okay, you've got me on that one. Do we know where the occupiers of the house are?"

"Nope. Not had a chance to investigate that side of things yet. We wanted to get the brigade back on the road again ASAP, so Julie and I have been busy taking down their statements. I'd take a punt that the house is empty, though, yet to be confirmed, of course."

"Glad to see my guy got here promptly to erect the marquee." Gerrard held out his hand.

Hero glanced up, and a few drops of rain landed on his face. "Something to be thankful for, I guess. Julie and I will begin the search of the house. We'll leave you to it."

"Good. My advice would be to keep out of the cellar."

Hero snorted. "That's a no-brainer."

Together, he and Julie went up the stairs. Julie felt the need to arm herself with her pepper spray canister, just in case. They dipped into each room. Although they were still furnished, the house was empty of all occupants.

"This is sick," Julie commented.

"I'm not with you?"

"There's obviously been a family living here. You know, kids as well as adults, and yet…"

"We have a dead body and what amounts to a blood bank in the cellar."

"Exactly." Julie entered the children's bedroom and removed one of the books from the shelf. "Age four to five."

Hero scanned the room and nodded. "I agree. Maybe the corpse on the barbecue is one of the kids."

Julie dropped the book on the floor then picked it up. "Don't say that. The thought of a child suffering in that way sends shivers running up my spine."

"And there was me thinking you hated kids."

"I don't hate them as such. Rob and I have discussed the issue, and we've agreed the world will be a better place if we don't add to the population."

"Yeah, most people think having kids is a breeze. It ain't, it's hard work and it's a drain on your energy most of the time."

"But rewarding all the same, right?"

Hero nodded. "Yep, I wouldn't be without my three. They definitely keep me on my toes, though."

"Oh, I thought Fay was in charge of most of the child-rearing responsibilities?"

"All right, there's no need for that. I do my share when I get home at night, don't you worry."

"I believe you," she replied.

The way she said it had Hero doubting that she believed him. He could argue the toss with her for hours but knew there'd be little point in that. Once Julie got an idea into her head, that was it. There was no changing her.

"Let's have a quick shufty through their things, see if we can find any clues as to where the family has gone."

"I don't think there'll be much in here. Maybe it would be better to start in the main bedroom first."

Hero nodded. "I'll do that, you search in here."

Julie's face was a picture of annoyance and frustration. Hero forced down the chuckle threatening to escape, smiled and left the room. He went along the hallway to what appeared to be the master bedroom with its en suite visible in the left-hand corner. He rifled through the chest of drawers—all four of them were empty. He moved on to the bedside tables. Again, both of these drew a blank. He slid open the wardrobe door. Although the rails were bare, a shoebox sat at the back of one of the shelves above. He withdrew it and opened the lid. Inside, he found personal memorabilia, old photos, and small gifts which the kids had clearly made themselves for Mummy and Daddy.

"Interesting, let's hope we gain something from this," Hero mumbled.

"What's that?" Julie appeared in the doorway.

He walked towards her and showed her the contents. "Exhibit A. There's got to be something in here of use."

Julie shrugged. "You'd think so. Strange that the family left it behind for us to find, don't you think?"

"Possibly. It was at the rear of the shelf. Maybe the wife is small and couldn't see it."

"Plausible," Julie added, frowning. "Nothing in the kiddies' room. Want me to help search in here or shall I make a start on downstairs?"

"Go downstairs. I'm nearly through in here. Just the en suite to check. Have you been in the bathroom?"

"No. I'll do that now."

"There might be the odd toothbrush lying around which we can grab for DNA purposes."

"Going now." Julie raced into the hallway.

Hero dipped into the en suite and was disappointed to find it stripped of anything personal except for a small bottle of shampoo sitting in the shower enclosure.

"Nothing in the bathroom, I'm heading downstairs," Julie shouted from the hallway.

"I'll be down in a minute."

He searched the en suite cabinet. Nothing in there either, only a clump of dust in the corner. Deflated, he went back downstairs to find Julie hunting through the cabinet in the lounge. "Anything?"

She shook her head. "Clear so far. Good job you found that box because I think they've been pretty thorough clearing out everything else."

"Let's not lose hope just yet, we still have the kitchen and office to search."

Julie nodded. "The office could prove beneficial."

"I'll take a punt with that then and leave this room to you."

The office was located a few doors down. The large desk and a mahogany bookshelf were the only items of furniture left in the room. Hero hunted through the desk drawers, which again left him disappointed.

Footsteps in the hallway drew his attention.

Gerrard popped his head round the door. "There you are. I have to say the firemen did well to spot the bone and ring you guys. It's going to take us a few days to gather all the evidence from the barbecue. We're going to take it all away and do it at the lab. How are you doing?"

"Nothing so far. Actually, that's a lie, sorry. I found a box of memorabilia in the main bedroom. Looks like they've been thorough in clearing out everything else apart from a few pieces of furniture."

"Strange they've left that, don't you think?"

Hero shrugged. "I'm guessing this place is probably rented. They took their personal stuff and did a moonlight flit."

Gerrard's eyes widened. "Good news for you. If nothing else it means there'll be a paper trail."

"Indeed. I know I'm asking a lot, but is there any way of knowing whether the victim was male or female yet?"

"Not so far. I should be able to give you something in the next few days. I want it to be as accurate as possible. I'd hate to give you duff info. You know me, ever the perfectionist."

"That's true. I'll leave that with you. Are you going to start in the cellar now?"

"Yep. Stating the obvious, I'd say by the blood spatter on the walls, the victim was bludgeoned before they lost their life."

"How accurate is that?"

"I'm willing to put my career on the line and say I'm seventy-five percent certain. I hope that's the case; either that or the person was hacked to death while they were still alive."

Hero's mouth turned down at the sides. "Don't say that, my damn legs have gone all weak now."

"You always were a bit of a softie. Hard on the outside and squishy on the inside."

"I'm human. Unlike some I could mention."

"Don't start on me. I love my job."

"I couldn't do it. Cutting up dead bodies, day in day out."

"It's the satisfaction of those dead bodies telling us how they perished that keeps me going."

"Not your morbid fascination then? Who'd have thought it?" Hero chuckled, earning himself a look of contempt from Gerrard.

"Think what you will. I have a murder scene awaiting my expert appraisal." He flounced away from the door.

Hero took pleasure in winding the pathologist up, just like he did Julie. They were easy targets after all.

He left the office and went in search of his partner. He found her going through the drawers in the kitchen. "Anything?" he asked.

"Plenty of kitchen appliances and gadgets. Shall we get SOCO to dust for prints and bag them up?"

"Maybe a few items. Such as a few knives, maybe some cutlery. That should do the trick. Make a list for the landlord."

"You're thinking this place is rented then?"

"Don't you?"

Julie twisted her mouth. "Hadn't really thought about it until you mentioned it. Makes sense. Want me to see if I can find out?"

"We can do that in the morning. For now, I think we should see what a few of the neighbours have to say before it gets too late."

"Do you want me to gather the equipment first?"

"Yes. Gerrard and his team are starting on the cellar. I'll knock on the immediate neighbours' doors. Do we know which one rang it in?"

"A couple of them did. Try the one on the right. I think the occupier is a Mrs Cappol."

"Great. I'll make a start, and you can join me when you've finished in here."

He left the house and headed for Mrs Cappol's. The woman in her sixties, with a head full of rollers, answered the door within seconds of Hero ringing the bell.

"Come in, excuse the state of me. Oh gosh, I'm thinking this is bad if the police have turned up. You should have seen the blaze. I had to ring the fire brigade. I was worried about the bloody thing spreading. What the hell were they burning anyway?"

"Is there somewhere we can sit and have a chat, Mrs Cappol?"

"In the kitchen. I take it you'll be wanting a nice cup of strong tea? I know I could do with one."

"A coffee for me, if it's not too much trouble."

"Come with me. I'll see what I can find in the cupboard. We're tea drinkers in this house."

"Then tea is fine, honestly, don't go to any trouble on my behalf."

"Nonsense, I've got some coffee somewhere. It's probably well past its sell-by date, though."

"Tea is fine, don't worry."

Mrs Cappol pulled out a chair at the kitchen table as she passed. "Sit down, love. I won't be a tick." She pottered around and filled the kettle.

Hero sat in the chair and extracted his notebook from his pocket. "When did you notice the fire?"

"It was when I went up to bed. I drew the curtains in my bedroom and thought, blooming heck, what in God's name is that? I rang my old man first—he's on nights at the local factory. He thought I was being foolish. I didn't think so, hence me calling the brigade out. Must be bad if they involved you. What is it, some kind of arson?"

Hero sighed. He really didn't want to burden the woman any more than was necessary. However, he needed information about the family. "Not really. At the moment we're unsure what's going on. Maybe you can tell me who lives there?"

"Oh, I see. A young couple and their two children. Successful they are, judging by the cars they drive. Not had much to do with them really."

"Have they lived here long?"

Hero poised his pen, waiting for her response.

"Let me think." She poured the boiling water into two mugs, added a splash of milk and asked, "Sugar?"

"Two, please. I've cut down recently."

"It's not good for you. Too much sugar in our food these days. When you think back to during the war, not that I was alive then. Saw a programme about it the other day, I did. The poor kids had no idea what a bar of chocolate was like until the Yanks joined the war."

"I think I saw the same programme. Hard to believe, wasn't it? Sorry, have they lived there long?"

"Around two years or so, off the top of my head, that is."

"What about their names?"

"I had a letter delivered here once for them. What was it now?" She handed Hero his mug and sat in the chair next to him. "It began with a K. A short name, it was."

"Knight, Kit, Knox?"

"Knox rings a bell. Yes, I think that was it. You are clever."

Hero's cheeks heated with the compliment. "Knox. What about their first names?"

"Sorry. It was initials on the letter from what I can remember. I'd be lying if I told you what those were. I saw it wasn't for me and took it over there as soon as possible. Told the postie off the next day, too. Young lad, he was, always got those headphones on while he delivers the post. Can't be good for them, can it? Not paying attention to the roads when they're going round these estates?"

"No, I agree. What about the children? Did you manage to catch their names at all?"

"No. They were quite young. I always saw that older girl with them. Oops, I should have mentioned her, she slipped my mind for a moment. Pretty girl. I've seen her walking past recently and noticed that she'd lost a fair bit of weight. Probably anorexic, you know what teenage girls are like about watching their weight these days."

"A teenager, you say. Can you give me a better description?"

Mrs Cappol mulled the question over for a few seconds, a pained expression on her face. "Not really. Brunette, thin and pretty. I know, my observations are useless. Hubby always says the same thing."

"Don't be so hard on yourself. It's better than working with nothing. Maybe you'll think of something else during our chat. No pressure from me, how's that?"

She held her crossed fingers in the air and nodded.

"This young woman, how long had she been at the house?"

"Around the same time, although, thinking about it now, I don't think I noticed her when the family moved in. Maybe she was an elder daughter who was away at university and only visited now and again. On second thoughts, the couple were too young. Maybe a sister or niece then perhaps. Damn, here I go again, waffling on. Hubby always has a go at me about that. Sorry."

"You're fine. I'm keen to hear what you think. It's not like we have anything else to go on at the moment." He jotted down some notes and then asked, "Did you ever see any other visitors come to the house?"

"Not that I can remember. I didn't think it odd at the time, but now you've mentioned it, isn't that a little strange?"

"Possibly. Although, my wife and I don't tend to get that many visitors, only immediate family, like my mother and my twin sister."

"Twins! How wonderful. Are you close?"

"Very, always have been. We joined the TA, sorry, the Territorial Army together. Had some fun doing that, I can tell you. Now, my sister has been with the police a couple of years. She's already working her way up the ladder. No doubt she'll be a higher rank than me soon. She's also keen on bossing me around, given the opportunity."

"How great is that? Family is so important, isn't it? Unfortunately, hubby and I were never able to conceive any kids. I feel like I've missed out in life. As if God dealt me a raw deal."

"Sorry to hear that. I have three. Twin girls, and I adopted my wife's son. Couldn't you have gone down the adoption route?" Hero found it exceptionally easy opening up to the woman for some strange reason.

"Mr Cappol point blank refused to entertain the idea. Said he didn't want the DNA of a possible murderer under our roof. Absurd, I know. But once he gets a daft idea in his mind there's no shifting him. Silly bugger, he is."

"I'm sorry. From my point of view, all I can say is how rewarding it's been to have been Louie's father over the years. His own dad wasn't, how shall I say this, appreciative of the boy's value in this world."

"Then I'm glad you stepped in to take care of him. It takes a real man to take on another man's child the way you have. You must be a very special human being indeed."

Hero's cheeks warmed again under her admiring gaze. "Not really. Louie and my wife came as a package. I have no regrets.

Anyway, getting back to the job in hand. I know I'm asking a lot here, but I don't suppose you know what jobs the couple had, do you?"

She shook her head slowly. "No. Like I said, I wasn't that friendly with them really. Thinking about it, he tended to stay at home more than the wife. That's the only thing that truly struck me as being odd about them."

"Interesting, okay, at least that's something to go on. Maybe he worked from home. I noticed there was a study in the house. Again, I'm probably asking a lot of you here…I don't suppose you remember any details about the cars they drove?"

"She had a smart 'normal' car as I call it, and he had one of those larger models which would fit the whole family in. That's as much as you're going to get out of me about that, I'm afraid. Cars don't interest me in the slightest. I don't even drive, you see."

"Not a problem, hopefully one of the other neighbours will be able to fill in the blanks for me. Is there anything else you think I should know?" He took a large gulp of his cool tea.

Her gaze cast down to the linoleum floor, and she sighed. "I don't think so. I'm sorry I couldn't give you more information. Tough to do that when folks stick to themselves these days."

"It's fine. We'll find out what we need to know soon enough." He flipped his notebook shut, finished off his drink and left his chair.

Mrs Cappol saw him to the front door. He extended his hand for her to shake.

"I guess we'll find out soon enough what's going on," she said, a weak smile pulling her lips apart.

"I'm sure the journalists will ensure that happens. Thank you for talking to me today and for going out of your way to make me a drink."

"It was my pleasure. Good luck, take care of those three kids of yours," she called after him.

Hero waved and closed the gate behind him. "I will. Goodnight, Mrs Cappol."

He stood on the pavement, glancing at the houses around him, wondering where Julie was. He finally spotted her coming out of the house on the opposite side and went to meet her.

"Anything?" he asked.

"I've got a fair description of the man and woman. They had two kids, and there was another young woman in the house, unsure who she was though at present. You?"

"Less information than you got, but yes, there was a mystery woman in the house. She's lived there around the same amount of time as the Knoxes. What's your initial thoughts?"

"I don't like to speculate, you know that. Perhaps they had one of those open relationships, a threesome."

Hero whistled. "Whoa! You really want to go there so early on in the investigation?"

Julie shrugged, and her mouth twitched with disgust. "Anything's possible these days. Either that or the young woman was a nanny."

Hero nodded thoughtfully. "That's more like it. The neighbour I spoke to said the girl was always with the children. Another interesting fact for us to cling on to, is that she thought the girl had lost a considerable amount of weight recently. As if she was anorexic."

"By that I take it you want me to get in touch with the doctors in the area and to also see who was listed on the electoral roll."

"Yes. Why don't we just ring the council, see who was listed as being resident in the house on the council tax side of things first?"

"Suits me. It'll have to wait until the morning."

"I appreciate that. Anything on the couple's vehicles?"

"Not from the neighbour I spoke with," Julie replied. "I know, I know, I'll add the DVLA to my list of people to ring in the morning."

"You've got it. I think we should question a few of the other neighbours and then call it a night."

"Really? I'm prepared to work through, if necessary."

"If we had a true idea of what cars they used then I'd be over it like a rash, but we're up the creek without that information."

"True enough. Ploughing on then. I'll work on that angle with the next neighbour. Maybe someone has got a security camera we can tap into."

Hero glanced around quickly and shook his head. "Not from what I can see. I find that incredible, don't you?"

"Not really. Most people don't give a toss about anything these days."

Hero sniggered. "Ever the pessimist, Shaw."

She grunted and stormed off.

Hero cringed. It didn't take much to set his partner off, not these days. He pulled the collar on his woollen coat up around his neck, warding off a sudden gust of wind that had struck up. Thoughts of snuggling up to Fay filtered into his mind, but he swiftly booted them out of the way again.

He strode up the path to the next house. There was a light on in a downstairs window. Good, he hated waking people up just to ask a few questions they probably didn't know the answer to. ID in hand, he rang the bell.

A grey-haired gentleman opened the door. He was in burgundy pyjamas and wrapped in a grey velour robe. Hero chuckled inwardly. No doubt the man's wife had chosen his ensemble as most women tended to do, judging by how coordinated he was.

"Hello, sir. I'm DI Nelson of Greater Manchester Police. Would it be possible to have a brief word with you regarding an incident that has occurred across the road this evening?"

"Very well. Do you want to come in?"

"Thanks, it's turning a tad chilly."

The man stepped behind the door and welcomed Hero into the hallway. "I'm Maurice Baldwin, by the way."

"Pleased to meet you, sir. Can you tell me what you know about what's going on?"

"Pretty daft question. I was hoping you'd be able to shed some light on that for me. Rocked us, you know, when the firemen turned up. We were just going to bed. Me and the wife, that is."

"Is your wife able to join us?"

"Mandy, are you coming down? There's a copp…a policeman to see us."

Hero smiled. "I have no aversion to being called a copper, no need to feel embarrassed."

"Come through to the lounge, my wife won't be long."

Hero sat in the armchair, Mr Baldwin took the sofa, and they waited for Mrs Baldwin to enter the room.

"Sorry, I'm here now. This is awful, you lot coming around here at this time of night. What's it all about?"

"I can't say at present. Our initial assessment is that someone might have been assaulted at the property. I wonder if you can tell me what you heard regarding the incident."

"We were just getting ready for bed, you know, we let the dog out in the garden and then we secured the house and went upstairs. All of a sudden, it was mayhem, sirens and lights flashing everywhere," Mrs Baldwin said, squeezing her hands together in her lap.

"I see. So there was no commotion before the brigade showed up?"

The couple glanced at each other and shook their heads.

"No, not that we heard. What on earth has gone on? Assault you say? The wife, was she assaulted?" Mr Baldwin queried.

"We're unsure at present. The facts are very hazy to say the least. What we're aiming to establish is who lives at the property, or lived, should I say."

"Lived? Have they done a bunk then?" Mr Baldwin asked, scratching his goatee beard.

"Possibly. Again, we're trying to assess everything and build a picture. Did you know the couple? I believe their name is Knox. Can either of you confirm that?"

"I can, yes, it was Knox. Sadie and Leonard, I think. Don't quote me on that, though. They introduced themselves to us when they first moved in. Oh wait, hang on, I wrote it down in my address book." She left her seat and went in search of the book. Returning, she showed the page to Hero.

He jotted down the information. "Excellent information. What about their children? I don't suppose either of you know what they're called?"

"Funny names, sorry, I meant they were unusual names. The boy is

Willow, and the girl's name has slipped my mind, to be honest. All I know is it begins with an A, if that helps?"

"It's better than nothing. Thank you. What age are the children?"

Mrs Baldwin puffed out her cheeks and chewed on her lip. "Difficult to say, three and four, maybe five and four. Around that age anyway."

"One of your neighbours also mentioned that there was another young lady living at the residence. Do either of you know much about her?"

Mrs Baldwin jumped in first. "I'm at home most of the day, signed off ill from work because of my nerves; this isn't helping much… anyway, I used to see the girl down the park with the kids. She seemed happy enough most of the time, although looking deeper into her soul I could see there was a tinge of sadness to her, that she appeared to be putting a brave face on."

"Mandy, stick to the facts. You don't know that's true, love."

"Hush now, Maurice, the nice policeman doesn't want to hear us squabbling. If he chooses to ignore what I've said then so be it. I'd rather voice my opinion on the lassie than say nothing."

"You've done the right thing. A little insight into a person at this stage can make all the difference during an investigation. I appreciate every particle of information if it helps us to build a case. What about her name?"

Mrs Baldwin vigorously shook her head. "Never heard that. Wait… the other day the little girl shouted Jacundy—sorry, that's what it sounded like to me anyway. She might have been a foreign nanny for all I know."

"A nanny? Is that what she is? You know that for sure? Okay, see, what you think might be useless information is turning out to be key clues for me to chase up. Someone told me this young woman appeared to have lost a lot of weight recently. Did you notice the same thing?"

"I think so. She's always with the children; I rarely see her by herself. And yes, I've noticed her failing health. I said to Maurice the girl appeared gaunt, her cheeks sallow, and her legs are like matchsticks, painfully thin, as if they'd break in an instant."

Hero jotted down the information. "I see. She wasn't always that thin then?"

"No, if anything she was on the tubby side when she showed up here. Maybe she had a new boyfriend and wanted to lose weight for him? A guess on my part."

"Did you ever see her with anyone other than the children?"

"No, can't say I have. See, I do talk a lot of rubbish sometimes," she added with a shrug.

"Nonsense, there's no such thing, not when we're dealing with an incident of this magnitude." Hero cringed—he realised he'd said too much.

"What's gone on over there? We can't see from our side of the road. Why are the firemen here, and you for that matter?"

"There was a fire in the back garden. We're here because the house was empty which has raised everyone's suspicions." Hero hoped he'd supplied enough to prevent the couple from asking further questions which he would struggle to answer.

"I see. Very strange. I wonder why they aren't at home. Not like them to go out at night, especially taking the children with them. Not that I profess to know the ins and outs of what that family gets up to, of course."

"A moonlight flit, I said as much earlier," Mr Baldwin chipped in.

"I can neither deny nor confirm that at this stage, although the likelihood of you being right is what's going through my mind at present. I don't suppose either of you knows what cars the couple drive?"

"By that you want to know the make and model and the plate numbers, I take it?" Mr Baldwin asked.

Hero poised his pen over a blank page in his notebook. "That would be an immense help, sir."

"Ah, there lies the problem. I'm not good at remembering plates, but she drove a Vauxhall, and he always went around in one of those people carrier thingies. If I said it was a Ford Galaxy, I don't think I'd be far off the mark. Grey, it is."

"That's brilliant, thank you. And the Vauxhall?"

"A midnight blue, although it could have been black. The eyesight isn't what it used to be, not at my age."

Hero smiled. The man wasn't that old, not compared to how old his father had been when he'd passed away. Thinking about his father brought a lump to his throat. He gave a slight cough. "I'd say your observation skills were very much intact, sir. Did you see any visitors show up at the house?"

The couple shook their heads.

"No, never. Most people get at least one visitor now and again, surely, but not them. I did notice that and thought it was strange," Mrs Baldwin admitted.

"Okay, I think that's covered everything now. I really appreciate you taking the time this evening to speak with me. What you've divulged will help to get the investigation underway."

"Glad to have been of some help." Mrs Baldwin smiled awkwardly as she stood.

Hero handed her one of his cards. "If you think of anything else, don't hesitate to get in touch. Thank you again."

The couple waved him off. Hero went in search of Julie. She was still talking to one of the neighbours on the doorstep.

She said farewell and joined him. "Why is it you always get invited into a property and I have to freeze my bits off outside?"

"My friendly manner might have something to do with it."

"Bloody charming, that is. I try and smile at these people. It's not easy for me, you know that."

"I know. So don't complain when people take offence and refuse to let you in then. What have you got, anything new?"

"Nope, nothing of importance. The old guy was intent on telling me all his woes about losing his wife last year and how he's struggled ever since."

"Wow, and you stood there listening to him without a bean of compassion?"

Julie hitched up a shoulder. "We've all lost someone in our lives.

You just have to shake off the grief and get on with things. You know that as well as I do."

"Julie, Julie, Julie!"

"What? Forget it, I can do without the lecture."

"Okay, as it's getting late, we'll let things lie there. I've got the makes of the cars and a possible lead on the young woman—a nanny."

Julie bashed her temple with her fist. "I should have trusted my instinct. It fleetingly crossed my mind for a brief second a while back then scampered off again."

"It's late. Don't stress about it. Back to the car where it's warmer. Let's get the station on the lookout for the cars for now."

5

*H*ero finally climbed into bed again around two in the morning. There was very little he could do at the station until the rest of the team were in and they had access to the usual places for their investigation, such as the council and DVLA. That was the frustrating part when crimes took place at night.

When the sun rose, Fay moaned and stretched beside him. "What time did you get in?"

"Two or thereabouts. You were out for the count."

She leaned over and kissed him. "And you're such a sweetheart for not waking me."

"My life wouldn't be worth living if I had, right?"

"Well, that's true. How did things go?"

He sighed. "I think this is going to be a nasty one—it's already that. I won't go into details about what we discovered. We're on the hunt for a family now. After interviewing the neighbours, the family seems elusive, not much to go on really."

"Was there a body at the house?"

He nodded and said reluctantly, knowing how squeamish Fay could be, "The remains of one. Don't ask me to say more, it'll give you nightmares, hon."

"Don't tell me. My life is complicated enough looking after the three terrors. I'd rather not have to combat dealing with nightmares on top. Talking of the children, I suppose I'd better make a move. What time are you going in today?"

"Usual time. We need to hit the phones early, gather as much information as we can and get these bastards caught swiftly. I'm going to jump in the shower now, if that's okay?"

"Since when do you have to ask my permission?" she replied, tutting.

They shared another kiss, then Hero flung back the duvet and crossed the room to the en suite. Fay let out a wolf whistle behind him.

He glanced over his shoulder. "Do you mind?"

"Not in the slightest. The view from here is wonderful. You're still as trim as the day I met you, thank goodness. So many men go to pot once a woman has snared them."

"I need to keep fit. Can't have the baddies running rings around me, can I?"

He continued his journey and ran the shower. Standing under the hot water, his mind was already on his day job, the order of events he'd need to deal with once he arrived at the station. After showering, he completed his morning ritual by cleaning his teeth and having a quick shave. He preferred his clean-shaven look to the trend of sporting a beard—facial hair wasn't for him at all.

He dressed in his navy-blue suit and ran downstairs to assist Fay with getting the kids ready for school. "Morning, munchkins, how are we today?"

The twins issued a toothy grin.

"Ready for another day at school, Daddy," Zoe replied.

Zara nodded, agreeing with her sister, and shovelled a mouthful of cereal.

Louie sat there staring at his bowl of cornflakes. Hero ruffled his hair. Louie pulled away, annoyed by the display of affection.

"Hey, what's wrong with your face?" Hero asked, a little concerned by his stepson's reaction.

"Nothing. Can't a person have a little peace and quiet before they start their day?"

Hero laughed. "Are you for real? You're eleven, Louie, you sound like a thirty-year-old."

"Stop teasing the lad, Hero," Fay butted in.

"I'm not. Louie, is everything okay with you? Do you need to have a chat about something?" Over the years, Hero had tried to enforce upon his children the necessity to be open with him and Fay. Up until now, they'd all managed to achieve that aim.

His gaze cast down at his breakfast, Louie said, "It's fine, Dad. Stop worrying. I'm just not in the mood for you winding me up this morning."

"Okay, if that's the way it is, son, although, in my defence, I wasn't really winding you up, not this time. You know you can always speak to either me or your mother openly about anything that's troubling you, don't you?"

"I do, and nothing, I repeat, nothing is troubling me right now, so there's no need for you to worry about me. Mind if I get on with my breakfast without any more hassle?"

Hero pulled a face at Fay and mouthed, "Consider me told."

She rubbed his arm and winked at him to reassure him.

"I'll be leaving soon. Does anyone need a lift?" he asked the children, trying to ease it for Fay.

"Don't worry, I've got it covered. My morning is pretty stress-free, or it should be. You head off."

Hero munched on his slice of toast and washed it down with the remains of his coffee, then he bent down and kissed each of his children on the head. A twinge of hurt ran through him when Louie ducked to avoid a kiss. Fay silently warned him not to react. She kissed him and sent him on his way.

Fifteen minutes later, Hero drew up in his allocated place at the station and ventured inside the old craggy building. "Morning, Ray. How's it diddling?"

The desk sergeant smiled and nodded. "Fair to middling, sir, yourself?"

"About the same. I don't suppose you have anything for me?"

"If you're asking if we've made any arrests overnight to do with the new case, then I'm going to disappoint you."

"Okay, it was worth a shot. Anything at all?"

"Zero, sorry, sir. I've got my lot keeping an eye out on the streets, but nothing so far."

"Oh well, looks like we'll have to figure things out the hard way, as usual."

"No change there, sir," Ray agreed.

Hero trudged upstairs and walked into the incident room to find Julie and Sally already at their desks. "Morning, ladies, I see the men are slacking once again."

"As usual, nothing new there," Julie grumbled.

"A coffee would be nice, partner," he said, pushing his luck and Julie's mood to the limits.

She glared at him and then got to her feet. "Sally?"

"I'm fine, thanks."

Julie returned carrying two cups. She handed one to Hero and placed the other on her desk.

"Thanks, I owe you one. I'll be in my office. Give me a shout when the others show their faces."

"You owe me more than one," Julie muttered.

Awaiting him was the usual dross—an Everest proportion of paperwork needing his attention. He groaned and plonked himself in his chair ready to tackle the onerous chore. First, he took several sips of coffee, hoping the caffeine rush would kick in and lend a hand.

The paperwork included several notifications from head office about the way the paperwork for each investigation was to be handled in future. "Sodding changes, bane of my bloody life. I can sense a rollicking coming my way when I choose to ignore them for a few weeks. All in favour of causing chaos at the other end."

"You know what they say?" Julie asked, startling him.

"What?"

"First sign of madness. What I want to know is if you ever respond to yourself." She cracked a smile which vanished as soon as it stretched her lips apart.

"Occasionally, I get more sense that way."

Julie's eyes narrowed. "I popped in to tell you the team are all here, and all you can do is fling insults at me."

"Whoa! I did nothing of the sort. It's going to be one of those days, is it? Rein your temper in a little, will you?"

"Sorry. That's what comes from not having enough sleep. I didn't drop off until about six, and then my bloody alarm went off around seven."

"I, on the other hand, managed to get back to sleep as soon as my head touched the pillow."

"Good for you. Men never seem to have much trouble in that department. I've had a word with Him upstairs and asked if I can come back as a man next time. You have life easy, well easier than most women I know anyway."

"Ya think? We'll agree to differ on that one. I'll be out in a tick."

Julie flounced out of the room. He heaved out a long-suffering sigh and downed the rest of his drink.

He tidied away his paperwork and left the office. Picking up the marker pen at the whiteboard, he announced, "Okay, team, gather around." He jotted down the address and the make of the vehicles, along with the names of the family members. "This is what we have so far—it's not much. Let's go cautiously on the names until we have something solid to cling on to. Our main aim is to concentrate on the vehicles—track those down and we've got them. Easy, right? We'll see about that. Nothing is easy these days. What we're looking at is trying to find the Knox family: mother, Sadie; father, Leonard; and their two children. The boy is called Willow, and the girl is called something beginning with an A, which could be anything at this stage." He paused, allowing his thoughts to shuffle into position. At the moment, they were bouncing around all over the place.

"I'll get on to DVLA, get clarification of the vehicles and who they're registered to," Julie volunteered.

Criminal Actions

"Want me to check with the council, sir?" Sally asked.

"Brilliant, ladies. If we can get that information ASAP we should be laughing. One other thing we need to concentrate on is the other adult at the residence. There's a firm belief the young woman could be the nanny. We also need to check on the kids. See what school they attended, if any. Speculation is that they're around three and four, maybe even five tops. Sounds like they might have been enrolled in a playschool. Someone check into that for me? Jason?"

"Will do, boss."

"Okay, that leaves background checks and the CCTV footage to cover. Jason, I need you to work on that angle with Lance. Do the school search first, if you would?"

"Yes, boss. On it now."

The team got on with the tasks in hand. Hero knew what he had to do next—inform the DCI what they were dealing with. "I'll be back once I've brought the guv'nor up to date."

He walked the length of the long grey corridor and rapped on the door.

"Hello, Hero. What can I do for you?" Sandra, the DCI's PA asked with a smile.

"New case. I need to bring the boss up to speed. Is he free?"

"Let me check, be right back." She left her desk and entered the door to her right, closing it gently behind her. She reappeared and opened the door wide for him to pass. "Go right in."

"Ah, Nelson. What's this new case about then? Take a seat."

"Thanks, sir. I was called out to a bit of a gruesome find last night. Not much to go on as yet. Looks to me like the family has left the house. We're in the process of trying to track the vehicles down to corroborate that at present; we're unsure who the corpse belongs to."

DCI Cranwell tapped his cheek with his pen. "Back up a second. Unsure who the corpse belongs to. Surely you know if the person is male or female?"

"Sadly not, sir. The body was disposed of in a lit barbecue. The fire brigade was called when a neighbour spotted the barbecue on fire in the back garden. One of the firemen saw a bone on the grill and shouted for them to stop. That bone was from a human—too big to belong to an animal—that was his understanding. Good job he had his wits about him, that's all I can say."

"Too much detail, I can feel my breakfast rising. What are you doing about finding the residents?"

"The usual, boss. I've actioned the team. It's a waiting game now until we have all the relevant information to hand. In the meantime, we've got an alert on two vehicles. Shaw is in the process of contacting DVLA to get the licence numbers. That'll make a difference, I hope."

"Two vehicles?"

"The husband's and the wife's. There were no vehicles left at the residence, therefore we have to presume the family has taken off in both cars. Again, at this stage this is purely supposition on my part."

"Working on that gut of yours again, Nelson?"

"It's the best I can do in the circumstances, sir."

"If, as you say, the family has absconded, then who was burning on the charcoal?"

"As far as I can tell, the family possibly employed a nanny. My guess is it could be her. Or perhaps the husband took a fancy to the au pair and killed the wife. Who knows?" He shrugged.

"When will you know?" Cranwell demanded harshly.

"How long's a piece of string, boss? I suppose once the pathologist has done his bit then we'll have a better idea who the victim is and we can go from there."

"And that's likely to be?"

"A few days yet. As I said, there's very little of the victim left for him to deal with. I'd hate to put pressure on him to come up with a result."

"But you're going to anyway, aren't you?"

Hero sighed. "If that's what you want, sir?"

"It is. What else happened last night?"

"Well, we discovered a lot of blood in the cellar of the house. We suspect the murder took place there. Again, SOCO will have their work cut out for them, analysing the blood spatter et cetera."

The DCI shook his head. "You mentioned a family. Are you telling me there are kids involved in this shocking crime?"

"After speaking to the neighbours, yes, two young kids, ages three to five."

"My goodness. Any chance one of the kids...you know?"

"Could be the victim?"

"Yes."

"I don't think so, sir. The length of the bone was akin to an adult human as opposed to a child."

Cranwell exhaled a relieved sigh. "Thank fuck for that. I've seen my fair share of kids' deaths over the years and could do without having another one on my patch."

"I agree. I'm hoping the PM will come back soon. Until then we're scuppered as far as IDing the victim is concerned."

"Have you arranged house-to-house yet?"

"I intend doing that today. Although, Shaw and I questioned all the immediate neighbours late last night."

"Well, you seem to have everything under control. Keep me abreast of how things develop."

Hero stood. "I will do, sir. Hopefully, we'll get things wrapped up within the next few weeks."

"Nothing like adding a little stress to the proceedings. Ensure all the proper procedures are followed and PACE is actioned correctly. I'm hearing too many unnecessary screw-ups are happening amongst your fellow officers right now. Don't make me come down heavy on you, got that?"

"As ever, sir, I'll do things by the book."

"Hmm...I can recall a few dubious cases you've dealt with in the past, Nelson. Up your game on this one."

Hero nodded and left the room. He puffed out his cheeks as he closed the door.

"Tough meeting?" Sandra asked sympathetically.

"The usual. It's a hard case we're dealing with, so to be expected, I suppose. Enjoy your day, Sandra."

"You, too, Hero. I have every confidence in you achieving a great result."

"I wish I could share that confidence." He smiled, left the outer office and made his way back to the incident room. There was a buzz in the atmosphere. "Everything all right, gang?" He crossed over to Julie's desk.

"I have the car regs. Pleased to say that the information we've been given so far has been good. The cars belong to Sadie and Leonard Knox. I've passed on the regs to the desk sergeant—he's going to ensure his team is up to speed. It's only a matter of time before we grab the bastards, boss."

Hero gave the thumbs-up. "Excellent news. Once we get the cars identified on CCTV and are aware who's driving the vehicles then I'll presume we're making some headway on the case, not until. If the wife is driving then that means the nanny is the victim and vice versa. Julie, I want you to ring all the nanny agencies in the area. There can't be that many in Manchester, I wouldn't have thought so anyway. Let's try and at least put a name to this young woman and go from there."

Julie nodded. "On it now."

"Do you mind if I add something to that?" Sally asked.

"Go on, Foxy," he said, referring to her using the nickname she preferred at work.

"It might be worth a shot visiting the local park. If there are other nannies there, perhaps they can give us a little background on what went on in the house."

"Excellent idea. Anyone knows what time of the day nannies tend to meet up?"

Julie shrugged. "Nope, I'm inclined to think it would be later in the day, around end of school time."

"It depends how old the children are, I suppose," Foxy added.

"It's imperative we ascertain the true ages of the children and what type of schooling they had. Maybe they were home-schooled. Again, we're coming up with more questions than answers on this one. Let's work harder and smarter, guys. One thing we know for certain is that these bastards are getting away from us."

6

*S*everal hours and numerous cups of coffee later, the team came up trumps to a number of the enquiries. Foxy established that the young woman's name was Jacinda Meredith and that she was twenty. Jason spotted the cars travelling together, leaving Manchester on the A6 near Levenshulme. After that, the cars vanished from the spotlight. Hero sent Jason and Lance out to the location to have a scout around. They were still awaiting news from that.

Jason had also located the playschool the two children attended, and that was where Hero and Julie were heading now, to question the head. Leaving Foxy trying to piece together the Knoxes' backgrounds, which up to the point of them leaving the office was proving to be difficult.

Mrs Woodward was a petite lady with a squeaky voice. She had run the school for the last ten years and enjoyed her role with a passion, if her enthusiasm in which she spoke about the children in her charge was anything to go by. "Ah yes, the Knox children. April and Willow. They have only been registered with us for a few months. Quiet children, very well-mannered."

"Good to hear. Are they at school today?"

"Oh no. Mrs Knox rang me to say they had a family emergency

and had to visit relatives over the next few weeks. I'm not expecting to see them anytime soon."

"I see. Did Mrs Knox mention where they were possibly going?"

"No. Why, has something happened?"

"We're investigating an incident which took place at the Knoxes' residence. I'm afraid I can't tell you anything other than that for now."

A frown knitted her brow. "Are you telling me this incident concerned the children? It must do, otherwise, why would you be here?"

"A tenuous link. All we're trying to do is to build a picture of the family and their routines. The children attended your school daily?"

"Yes, Jacinda was in charge of dropping them off and picking them up because the parents are both busy people."

"What can you tell us about the three people you mentioned?"

They were standing in the school hallway.

"Why don't we go to my office? I can speak more freely there."

Hero nodded. He and Julie followed the woman down the wide hallway to the office situated at the end.

"Please, take a seat. I'll get their administration file."

Julie took out her notebook and poised her pen ready, while Hero sat fidgeting in the chair next to her.

"Here we are." Mrs Woodward sat and flipped open the manila folder. "According to my records, Mr Knox worked from home. He's a property developer, and Mrs Knox works for an auction house."

"That's very useful information, thank you. What about the nanny? I appreciate there will be nothing on file about her. I meant, did you know her at all? Possibly spoke to her when she dropped the kids off?"

"I try to make contact with the parents or the people they assign to pick up their children. Jacinda was a lovely girl, very inoffensive and always walking around with a smile on her face, until recently, I should say."

"Any reason for the change?"

"She told me she was missing her parents up in Scotland and was finding it difficult getting the time off work to visit them. I suppose that's the trouble when you have a live-in job. People tend to take you more for granted, see you as being at their beck and call all day."

"Is that what happened?"

Mrs Woodward shrugged. "I don't know. All I saw was a young woman seeming to get more and more depressed with each passing day. I try not to intervene unless I'm asked, so it was heartbreaking to witness her decline, to be honest with you. Has Jacinda gone with them? To look after the children?"

"We're unsure about that."

"Maybe the Knoxes have given her the time off to recharge her batteries with her parents up in Scotland."

"We'll try and locate them and find out. Did Jacinda ever mention if she enjoyed her job?"

"Oh yes, she adored April and Willow, treated them like her own. Very protective of them." She leaned over the desk and lowered her voice, "Truth be told, I think she treated the children far better than some of the parents I deal with. I've never once heard her shout at either of them. And well, I think the feeling was mutual. At the end of the day, they always ran into her arms. My take is, because of her age, the children probably regarded her as an older sister rather than a nanny."

"I see. That's really helpful. I don't suppose you know where she used to take them after school? Straight home or to a park perhaps?"

"The park around the corner; it was a daily ritual. Rain or shine, the children loved spending time there."

"What sort of students are they?"

Julie tutted beside him, and Mrs Woodward chuckled. "We don't tend to grade the pupils, if that's what you're asking. They're preschool age. Playschool is predominantly about preparing the children for what lies ahead of them, if you will. More about how to play and deal with each other, interaction skills. Manners are also important, although the parents must play their part as well in that."

Hero dipped his head, embarrassed. "Sorry, I should have thought about that."

"Do you have any children, sir?"

"Yes, three."

Mrs Woodward raised an eyebrow. "What are their ages?"

Julie snorted.

"My son is eleven and my twins are almost six. I know, that makes me sound like a bad dad now."

Mrs Woodward shook her head. "Not in the slightest. I can imagine your career isn't an easy nine-to-five job."

"You're not wrong there. My wife does all the heavy lifting where the kids are involved. I'm grateful about that, although I do sit down and play with the children at night, if I'm home. Ignore me, I'm digging myself deeper into a hole here."

Mrs Woodward laughed. "Not at all. It's nice to hear a father say that, if only occasionally."

"Okay, I think we've covered everything for now. I'll leave a card. If either of the Knoxes or Jacinda show up in the next few days, will you ring me?"

"I will. Shall I inform them that you wish to talk to them?"

"No, just ring us, and we'll take it from there. Thanks for taking the time out of your busy schedule to speak with us."

"It's a pleasure. Sorry I couldn't tell you where the family is heading."

"Did they say how long they were intending to be away?"

"Two weeks, maybe three." Mrs Woodward escorted them out of the office and back to the entrance where she shook their hands. "Good luck with your investigation."

"Thank you. I have a feeling we're going to need that."

They crossed the playground and jumped back into the car.

"It's looking more and more likely that the nanny is the victim." Hero inserted his key into the ignition and drove off.

"I'm still unsure about that."

"Why the uncertainty?"

Julie shook her head. "Can't put my finger on it, sorry."

"From what the head just told us, the girl was clearly depressed. Maybe the couple bullied her."

"Not sure how you come up with that. What if she was missing her family, like the head suggested?"

"True enough, especially a twenty-year-old. We need to locate the parents."

"Scotland is a pretty big place."

"There's no need for you to be sarcastic. Let's see if there are any nannies at the park."

"I doubt it at this time of day. All the kids will be in school."

"Worth a try. Some nannies have younger kids to care for, right?"

"If you say so."

I do! He left the car park and drove slowly to the next location which Julie had sourced on Google Earth. The park was relatively quiet, although there were a few women gathered around chatting over near the swings. A number of tiny children, around the age of two and three, were on the swings.

Hero fished out his ID and introduced himself and Julie. The five women seemed worried at first by the interruption.

"What's this about? We've done nothing wrong," a young blonde woman asked, clinging on to the toddler she lifted off the swing.

"Just a few questions, if that's okay with you?" Hero asked.

"About what?"

Hero smiled, trying to put the women at ease. "We're hoping to find out about a nanny in the area and wondered if you ladies could help us."

"Who?" the blonde demanded.

"Jacinda Meredith."

"Right, what's she done first? And then we'll tell you if we know her or not," the blonde said, glaring at Hero.

"She's not in any trouble, not as far as we know. All I'm trying to do is see what you good ladies know about her and if anyone knows where she might be right now."

"Is she missing?"

"Possibly. Do you know her?"

"Yes, she's a regular visitor to the park. Haven't seen her for a few days, thought she might be away on a mini-break. She's been going on about travelling up to Scotland to see her parents for the past six months or more."

"Okay. Any idea where that is?"

"What, Scotland?"

The other women sniggered at the blonde's attempt at humour.

"Ladies, can we cut the crap. This could be important. Just stick to the facts, we're busy people," Hero said.

The blonde snarled at them. "Get you, aren't we all?"

Hero grinned. "I'm sure. Perhaps you can give us a little insight into Jacinda's character?"

"Why? Tell us that first."

"I can't go into specifics. We're trying to find her to have a chat, we need her to help us with our enquiries."

"What enquiries?" The blonde persisted with her relentless questions.

Hero had to keep a tight grip on his temper. "We're investigating an incident which took place at the Knox residence yesterday. That's all I can say about it for now."

The women glanced at each other. Some looked far more concerned than others.

"Why am I getting the impression that hasn't come as a surprise to some of you?"

Another woman, dressed all in black with matching black hair and makeup, spoke up first. "We've been chatting amongst ourselves about Jacinda over the past few weeks."

"May I ask what these chats consisted of?"

"A few of us have been worried about her. She's lost a lot of weight in the last month or so, and the sparkle has gone from her eyes."

"Interesting. Did she give a reason for the changes?"

"No. She used to be really open with us, spoke all the time about the children and how she loved working for the family, but all that stopped. We tried to get out of her what was wrong—clearly something was, but she refused to let us in. What's going on, where is she?"

"The answer is, we don't know. We're conducting enquiries after a puzzling incident occurred at the residence."

"What type of incident? Oh God, she hasn't been hurt, has she?"

"I can't say any more than that. Does anyone know what part of Scotland she's from?"

"She mentioned 'just over the border' to me, that's all I know," the blonde replied.

"That's a start, thanks. Has she spoken about taking time off to any of you?"

"Always on about her need to go home, but also said it was impossible to get the time off with the family being so busy."

"Okay, is there anything else you think we should know? Wait... did she ever mention a boyfriend?"

The blonde tutted, and her eyes narrowed. "Nah, she dumped him when she first arrived, that's what she told me."

"I don't think she had time for a boyfriend," the girl in black replied. "None of us have got one. We're all just as devoted to the children in our care as she was."

"They take priority, right?" Hero asked.

"Most definitely. Once the kids get to be a little older, then I suppose things will change and we'll all be able to get our lives back."

"Good to hear. Okay, ladies, thank you for your assistance. We'll let you get back to work now. I'll leave you each a card. If you hear anything you believe I should know about, don't hesitate to contact me, day or night."

"When will we find out what this has all been about?" the girl in black asked.

"Soon enough. I have a feeling it'll be all over the news by this evening."

"Then what's to stop you telling us now?" blondie asked, frowning again.

Hero smiled and walked away to jeers from the women.

"You're such a tease, even when you don't realise it," Julie said on the way back to the car.

"*Moi*? I don't think so. I couldn't break the news to them. Besides, it hasn't been confirmed who the victim is yet."

"Not good that the group of women, and the head, all said that Jacinda seemed depressed. I wonder if she visited a doctor at all."

"Good shout. Can you look into that once we return? I'm going to see if I can track down her parents' address."

"You can't contact them, not yet."

"I know. That's not my intention, Julie. No harm in getting the address in case we need to speak to them in the near future, though, right?"

"I suppose. Did the pathologist say how long his tests were likely to take?"

"I'm thinking it could take him weeks to come up with an identification."

"Bloody hell, that long?"

"He's got to analyse what was left of the victim. No mean feat when there's very little left of the person in the first place."

"I know. What we truly need is a break. To find those two vehicles, and fast."

"Let's see what the rest of the team has managed to find out."

They returned to the station as Jason was parking his car.

"Anything in that area, Jason?" Hero asked, eager to find out about his mission to track down the Knoxes' cars.

"Nothing but a vast expanse of countryside, sir. I thought I'd come back here and search through the CCTV footage in the surrounding towns, see if they can help us ascertain the family's location."

"You get on with that. We'll talk more inside."

In the incident room, Hero drew the team's attention while Julie went in search of some coffee. "After speaking to several people today, I'm leaning towards the victim being Jacinda. By all accounts she had become withdrawn and depressed. A far cry from her usual bubbly self. I'm not inclined to make contact with her family just yet; we need to get her formally identified. How the heck the pathologist is going to do that is beyond me. Julie is going to contact the surgeries in the area, see if Jacinda was registered with a doctor, and Jason is going to try and trace the Knoxes' vehicles on the CCTV. Anything come up on the background checks? No, wait, we also learnt that Mr Knox is a property developer and Mrs Knox works at an auction house. Anything else, Foxy?"

"I was about to say the same, sir. Want me to chase up the auction house, see if she's shown up for work today?"

"If you would, although I won't be holding my breath on that one. I'll be in the office, doing some research of my own." He picked up his drink and sat behind his desk. It didn't take him long to trace a couple of families named Meredith. One was in the Outer Hebrides and the other in a small town called St Boswells, just over the border. He decided the latter was the likely choice and jotted down the phone number and address for when he was sure to need them. Next stop for Hero was to ring the pathologist. The more he pestered, the more probable he was to get the results quicker.

Gerrard seemed none too happy to hear from him. "I can't believe you're ringing up after less than twenty-four hours. For fuck's sake, give me a break."

"Sorry. There's a reason behind my call, I promise. Do you want to hear what it is?"

"Get on with it, man. I have my hands in a mixture of charcoal and ash and my nose is itching, making me more irritable than usual."

Hero laughed. "Sorry for your inconvenience. Right, through sheer expert detective work, we've established that the victim could be one of two people."

"I'm listening. It would be beneficial for both of us if you got to the point quickly."

"If you get off your high horse and listen, we'll get there even sooner."

"Hero..." Gerrard said in his renowned warning tone.

"Okay, by the look of things, either the nanny, Jacinda Meredith, or the wife, Sadie Knox, is the possible victim."

"Want to tell me how you've come to that conclusion?"

"If I must. The nanny has been depressed lately, unusual for her. And my take on the wife is, perhaps the nanny and the husband were having an affair and together they bumped the wife off."

"Okay. I'll throw this one into the mix as well. What if the wife and the nanny had an attraction to each other and ended up killing off the husband? Ha! You hadn't thought about that one, had you?"

"Fucking smartarse. No, I hadn't. Who knows what goes on behind closed doors these days?"

"Exactly. You should know by now never to jump to the obvious conclusion because invariably it turns out to be the wrong avenue to take."

"Well, that's put a damper on things, thanks for that, mate. My obvious question to you, therefore, is how long before you get the results."

"And there it is, in a nutshell. You're so damn easy to read. Piss off. You'll get them the second I have something I need to share with you."

"Gee, thanks for your professionalism, Gerrard. I'll leave you to it."

The line went dead.

7

"Mummy, my eyes are hurting, and it smells. Please stop!"

"Stop being such a baby, Willow."

"But you told me not to use that name."

Sadie—although now that name was forgotten and she now went under the name of Annette—continued rinsing the dye from her son's hair, turning him into a brunet, just like his sister. Like all of them. She hated this. Being forced to start over again. Yet another new identity. It was even harder now the kids were a little bit older. Having to think up new names and a genuine reason for having to change them was a real pain in the arse. The kids constantly badgered her with questions that she'd rather not answer. She'd even been tempted a couple of times to smack their backsides and send them to bed. However, she sensed that would make the transition so much harder in the long run.

The water ran clear. She dried her son's hair. They'd decided on Oscar for his name. His eyes were bloodshot, and he constantly blinked as if they were too sore to keep open.

"It'll soon be bedtime, children."

"Mummy, I miss Jacundy. Will we be seeing her soon?" May asked quietly.

From April to May. She thought it was a brilliant idea. Her husband hadn't been so keen on the transition at first. Thankfully, her daughter was delighted with the choice. She muttered the name over and over, Annette guessed to ensure it sank in quicker.

"Jacinda is taking a break. She'll join us once she's visited her family. Until then, I'll be looking after you. You like Mummy being with you all day, don't you?"

May and Oscar glanced at each other and shrugged.

"I think so, Mummy," May eventually replied.

There was nothing forthcoming from her brother, though.

"Oscar? Mummy asked you a question, at least have the decency to answer when I speak to you." She grabbed his thin arm, digging her fingers into his flesh.

"Ouch! Mummy, you're hurting me."

She released her grip, tugged her son into her arms and kissed his temple. "I'm sorry, sweetie." She wasn't. She was already bored with having the kids around her constantly. She was desperate to get back to work. "How about a big scoop of ice cream and chocolate sauce?"

"Yay! Yes, please, Mummy," they shouted in unison.

"Ah, bribery, it always works," her husband, now called Stewart, said light-heartedly from the doorway of the bathroom.

"Go and put your PJs on, kids. We'll meet you in the kitchen."

The children scurried out of the room and bolted along the small hallway. This house was much smaller than the one they had left. Still large by others' standards, but smaller all the same. Which might be the reason Annette was feeling the pressure of having the kids around her all the time.

"Everything all right?" Stewart asked, reaching out a hand to help her up from the floor.

She gathered the dirty towels and threw them at him, her anger coming from nowhere. "No, everything is *shit*. I didn't want to be taking this route again. I hate learning new names, giving the kids new identities. It's hard for them to adjust. It was easier for them the last time, they were so much younger then. Not only that, they're driving me nuts. All they do is whine and complain every hour they're awake."

He held up his hands in front of her, warding off the venom

spewing from her mouth. "Hang on a minute, take a breath and calm down, will you?"

"Calm down. Bloody hell, you utter those words one more time and I'll throttle you. We need another nanny, and pronto. I have to get back to work. I need more to stimulate me than chasing around after these two brats all day."

His eyes widened and then closed to a squint, his temper evident before he even opened his mouth. "Those *two brats* as you see fit to call them are your children. Over the years you've palmed them off onto the nannies we've employed. It wouldn't hurt you to look after them yourself for a few days until I organise another nanny. It's been less than twenty-four hours and you're already pulling your hair out. I suggest you try harder. Dig deep for the mother's instinct that you're obviously lacking and knuckle down to give them the love they're craving during this transition."

Annette took two steps forward and raised a hand to slap him. He caught her wrist and squeezed it, hard. He could be a bully when the call arose, just like her, but then, she'd known that from the day they'd met.

"Try it and it'll be the last thing you ever do, lady." He threw her hand down.

She chewed on her lip, an apology lingering on her tongue which failed to develop. Annette stormed out of the room and into the bedroom. She flung herself on the bed and released the pent-up emotions that had been threatening to emerge all day. She hated her life, a life she had no control over. Hated everything about being a mother. She didn't have it in her to listen to her kids wittering on every minute they were awake. Screaming at each other one minute and incessantly laughing the next. Most women would see her as fortunate to have two perfect kids. She saw them as a massive weight around her neck, a weight she was eager to get rid of.

He followed her into the bedroom and sat on the edge of the bed. "Please, love, none of this is easy, on any of us. Why fight the inevitable? Just accept that we both have to make sacrifices until we find another nanny to take over the reins. Don't let us fall out about this."

She turned over and stared at him. "You told me you'd sort another nanny out as soon as possible. We're still waiting."

"Give me time to get organised. It wouldn't be good to bring an outsider in during the early stages of the changeover. Let's get the kids used to their surroundings and their new names first. Leave it a day or two, and then I'll get on to the agency. Agreed?"

She closed her eyes and inhaled a calming breath. *A few days! How am I going to cope?* "I suppose I agree. Not too long, promise me that?"

He motioned for her to sit up and roughly hugged her. "I'm right about this, you'll see. Now, wipe your tears, put on your smiley face and get in that kitchen, wench."

Annette leaned back. It wasn't until she caught the glint in his eye that she realised he was joking. She slapped him around the top of the arm. "Don't leave it too long."

"I'll get on to the agency tomorrow afternoon. I'll also put an advert in the local paper, how's that? Tonight, we'll play the name game with the kids to ensure they understand what's going on. Okay?"

She nodded and slung her legs over the bed. They both stood. He hugged her again and whispered what he intended to do to her that night when they went to bed. There was a lightness in her step as they made their way into the kitchen.

The children thundered down the hallway after them the second they heard movement in the kitchen-diner.

Annette put on her happy face and dished up four large bowls of ice cream then slathered each one with chocolate sauce. It was a satisfying end to a trying day. As Stewart had suggested, they played the name game. Both children impressed them by not slipping up once.

"Right. It's time for bed, kiddiewinks. Kiss your mum goodnight, brush your teeth and jump into bed. We'll come and tuck you in soon."

The children hopped off their chairs, gave Annette a chocolate-covered, sticky kiss and darted up the hallway to their bedroom.

"See, that wasn't so bad after all, was it?"

She nodded, ashamed of her previous behaviour. "I suppose. You clean up in here, and I'll tuck them in."

"They'll need a bedtime story, are you up for that?"

"Yep, is the latest book they like beside the bed?"

"It is, I found it in one of the boxes this evening. They love *The Gruffalo*. We'll need to get more books in the series."

"You can sort that out, after you've employed another nanny."

"I can take a hint. Go, hurry, I'll clean up in here and will be waiting for you in the bedroom. I have a promise to fulfil."

"I'm going to hold you to that. Hopefully the kids will drop off soon, too exhausted to keep their eyes open after a manic twenty-four hours."

Annette left the kitchen. The children were sitting up in bed, *The Gruffalo* lying on the side of Oscar's bed, waiting for her.

"Mummy, sit here, next to me." Oscar patted the bed beside him.

She conjured up a smile, a weary one at that, and sat next to her son. "Snuggle under the quilt you two, and then I'll begin."

Ten minutes into the story, and both children were zonked out. She switched off the light and tiptoed out of the room. The light in the master suite was like a beacon to her needs. She pushed open the door to find her bare-chested husband sitting up in bed, one hand attached to the handcuff linked to the headboard behind. Her heart skipped several beats. She smiled and entered the room, locking the door behind her. Even if the kids screamed out because they were having a nightmare, she still wouldn't go to them. There were far more important things that needed satisfying tonight.

The following day, Annette stretched out and ran a hand across her husband's chest.

"Do you want an encore?" he asked sleepily.

The rattling of the doorknob put paid to that idea. "Hold that thought. I'm needed elsewhere."

He threw the duvet back, revealing his slim but muscular body. The body she adored and paid homage to every night. "I'll see to the kids, give you a break if you like."

She stretched her arms above her head and smiled. "That would be heaven. Thank you."

She drifted off to sleep and was woken by the aroma of freshly ground coffee. She sat up. Stewart placed a tray in front of her. "Wow, I didn't expect this. Breakfast in bed, what a treat."

"The best bacon sandwich around. Crispy bacon and thick granary bread slathered in butter. There's a serviette there to catch the drips. Enjoy. I'll get back to the kids; they're playing in their bedroom."

"I feel guilty, lying here like Lady Muck. You have work to do."

"Nonsense, a few days off will do me the world of good. Eat up before it gets cold and claggy."

She took a bite of her sandwich and swiftly mopped up the juices running down her chin. "It's divine and so thoughtful of you. I'm sorry I was such a bitch last night."

"Nonsense, we all get days like that. See you later."

She watched him leave the room, guilt and pride filling her in equal quantities. She was lucky to have a man like him beside her. Someone who was eager to satisfy her every need, unlike the other men who had filled her life before he'd come along. She was proud to call him her husband and was eager to ensure he remained with her for good. If that meant living a life on the run, then so be it. He was worth it.

8

It had been several frustrating days for Hero and the team. The pathology results took five days to come through. Now he was on the road, nearing the border with Scotland, about to deliver the news in person to the victim's parents. He was making the trip alone—couldn't stand the thought of being in the car for eight hours or more with his surly partner. Julie appeared relieved when he'd shared the news that he'd be venturing north by himself. He told her to keep going with the investigation in his absence. As yet, there was no news on either of the vehicles. Knowing what type of people they were dealing with, he'd come to the conclusion that the couple had probably attached false plates, to put them off the scent. He'd also concluded that they were dealing with intelligent people who had likely carried out other crimes of this nature in the past. Again, his team were trawling through the archives as he drove, in the hope of finding some clues to back up his notion.

According to his satnav, he was five minutes away from the Merediths' home. He'd rung ahead, ensuring the couple were at home to greet him. He'd been evasive in his request, skirting around the real issue behind his journey north. He wet his dry mouth with a gulp of Coke from the bottle next to him on the passenger seat and let out a gassy belch. "Pardon me. Jesus, why am I feeling so uptight about this?" He hated breaking such news to loved ones. Given the choice, he would have sent his partner to do the deed, except she would have delivered the news far more abruptly than him.

No, these people deserved to be told the imminent bad news with compassion, something he'd need to summon up from deep within.

The detached house emerged on the top of the hill. It was made from granite from what he could tell. It seemed cold and harsh to him. He sipped at the Coke again and then left the car, standing outside the front gate.

A suited man in his mid-forties opened the door. He shook Hero's hand and introduced himself as Thomas Meredith. "Come through to the lounge, the wife is in there."

Hero followed the man into a large living room. It was tidy, and on every surface there were photos of their pride and joy, their daughter, Jacinda. *Shit! This is going to be much harder than I first thought.*

"Hello, Mrs Meredith, pleased to meet you." Hero held out a hand.

She slipped hers inside and daintily shook it. "Thank you for coming all this way to see us. We're extremely nervous as to why you've come. I've tried to ring my daughter, but she's refusing to answer her phone. It's been that way for a few weeks now. I'm desperate for news about her. Please, don't keep us waiting any longer."

Hero sat on the sofa opposite the anxious woman and cleared his throat.

"Give the man a chance, Cathy. Here, can I get you a coffee after your long trip, Inspector?"

"It can wait, sir, thank you." Hero inhaled and exhaled a few short breaths and announced, "It is with sincere regret that I have some bad news regarding your daughter. Her body was found on Monday of this week."

Mrs Meredith screamed. Her husband stepped closer and placed an awkward arm around her shoulder.

She shrugged it off. "I told you something was wrong, you wouldn't have it…now my baby has gone. We could have helped her if only you'd listened to me. Now…it's too late. She'll never come home again. I'll never hold her in my arms…" She broke down.

Thomas stared at Hero, who was unsure what to say to ease the situation. He got the impression that the couple were no longer close, that something had died in their relationship, long before their daughter had. "I'm sorry. I came as soon as we were able to make a formal identification." He cringed, knowing that how he'd phrased his announcement was sure to invite more questions from the couple.

"Why so long?" Thomas asked, pacing back and forth in front of Hero.

"I'm sorry, I'd rather not go into details. The pathologist had to use your daughter's medical records to obtain an identification."

Cathy gasped and then broke down again.

"Meaning what? Oh God, forget I asked. Did someone do horrible things to her before she died?"

Hero nodded. "Please, don't force me to tell you. It's not pleasant. I wish the news was better for you, but it isn't. Are you up to answering a few questions?"

"Questions? You've just told us our daughter is never coming back to us and you expect us to answer your questions? What kind of heartless individual are you?"

"Thomas, don't you dare…" his wife cried.

Hero gulped down the lump in his tight throat. "I'm sorry, sir. Maybe I should go and come back another day."

Mr Meredith glared at him. "You'll do no such thing. I demand to know how my daughter died."

"I don't want to know the gruesome details, Thomas, don't force him to tell us," his wife pleaded.

"Then leave the room, woman. I'm entitled to hear how she died."

Cathy snatched a tissue from the box sitting on the table beside her and rose from her seat. "I'll be in the kitchen, making a pot of tea." She left the room, her shoulders sagging under her grief.

"Please, sir. Won't you take a seat?" Hero implored.

"I'm okay as I am. Get on with it, before she comes back. How did Jacinda die? And don't hold back. I'm a solicitor, I'm used to dealing with the dregs in our society and am fully aware how they operate."

"As you wish, sir. Your daughter was dismembered. Her body was found burning on a barbecue in the back garden of the Knoxes' residence."

"At the house where she was staying, *working*? How can that be? Where are Mr and Mrs Knox now? What do they have to say about this?"

"They were no longer at the residence. We believe they've absconded with their two children."

"Are you saying you believe they killed our daughter?" Thomas finally flopped into the chair next to him.

"Yes. They're essentially on the run. We've been searching for their two vehicles for days now without any luck."

"Have you put out a call for help through the media? No, of course you haven't, otherwise we would have seen it. What exactly have you been doing for the past five days, Inspector?"

"Everything possible, Mr Meredith, I can assure you. As you can imagine, without a true identification, our hands were tied to begin with, although that didn't stop us from questioning the Knoxes' neighbours."

"And what did they have to say about all this?"

"Enough to start our investigation. Sir, we haven't been sitting on our hands. As soon as we had an inkling who the victim might be, we upped our research et cetera."

"And when did you come to the conclusion it was our daughter?"

"I know where this is going, sir, you're going to reprimand me for not informing you personally. In my defence, I only deal in facts. There is no way I would have come to you to tell you that your daughter *might* have been killed. As soon as the pathologist confirmed the results of his examination this morning, I contacted you immediately and made arrangements to drive up here."

Mrs Knox entered the room, carrying a tray with three mugs, a teapot, a jug of milk and a sugar bowl. "Here you are." Her hands shook as she placed the tray on the coffee table.

Mr Meredith leapt out of his seat. "I'll do it, love, you sit down."

She glanced up at him and nodded then took her seat again. "I heard raised voices. More importantly, your voice, Thomas. I hope you haven't been giving the inspector a hard time?"

"No, dear."

Her eyebrows rose, and she shook her head. "I don't believe you. Did you ask how our daughter died?" She sniffled and extracted another tissue from the box.

"Yes, I assure you, you don't want to know."

"I'm sure. Inspector, do you have any idea who is responsible for our daughter's death?" Mrs Meredith asked, her voice quivering with emotion.

"I was just telling your husband that we believe the Knoxes are either responsible or they know who is. The couple are on the run with their two children."

Mrs Meredith stared at him. "No, I find that hard to believe. Jacinda had nothing but praise for the couple. And those children, well, she absolutely adored them and cared for them as if they were her own."

"When was the last time you spoke to Jacinda?" Hero asked, taking a sip of his tea, the second cup he'd drunk in the past few days, the taste still strange on his tongue after years of drinking nothing but coffee.

"A few months ago. On my birthday. It was a delight speaking to her, but I felt the conversation was a little strained. I told you, didn't I, Thomas? You told me not to worry, that she was probably under stress looking after the two children. So I let things lie. I wish I'd forced the issue and travelled down to Manchester now. Maybe she'd still be alive today if I'd dragged her home with me. That guilt is going to lay heavy in my heart for years to come, I promise you."

Fresh tears spilled onto her flushed cheeks, and Hero's heart went out to her.

"I'm so sorry, hindsight is a wonderful thing. Can I ask what took your daughter to Manchester in the first place?"

The couple glanced at each other and seemed anxious by the question. "Her boyfriend at the time persuaded her to go with him. He felt Scotland couldn't offer him anything and applied for a job in Manchester as a DJ in a nightclub down there. He urged Jacinda to go with him. She'd not long left school, was unsure which direction to go in workwise and took a punt. She got the job with the family about a month later. We were thrilled for her, although it signified the end of her relationship with Lenny."

"Why? Because it was a live-in position?"

"Yes. He wanted her all to himself. That was the true reason they went away together. She rang me after a week or so to tell me they were very much in love but it wasn't fulfilling her. I urged her to return home, but she was having none of it. Didn't want to be seen as a failure to her friends after she had bragged about going down south for a better life. It was a case of the grass not being that much greener, at least not with Lenny. Once she was settled with the family, her tone was lighter on the phone. I could tell she was enjoying life again."

"My enquiries have flagged up that she worked for the family around two years, is that correct?"

Mrs Meredith nodded. "Yes, give or take."

"And her calls stopped a few months ago? Did she give you a reason for that?"

"You mean did she warn us contact was going to halt?" Mrs Meredith asked.

"Yes."

"In a roundabout way. She said it was becoming increasingly difficult to ring home as the children were demanding more and more of her time. I didn't think that was right and told her in no uncertain terms that she should have a word with Mrs Knox for encroaching on her personal time. We're all entitled to time off, as you can appreciate. By what Jacinda said, she wasn't getting any time off. I suppose at first, I put that down to the perils of living under the same roof as her employers and them willing to take advantage of her good nature." She sighed and shook her head. "I can't believe I'm never going to hold her in my arms again." Tears cascaded, and Thomas left his chair to sit on the arm of the sofa to comfort his wife.

Criminal Actions

Hero sipped at his tea once or twice, giving the woman time to recover. "I appreciate how hard this must be. I can't thank you enough for opening up to me like this at such a sad time."

"We're doing it in the hope that our daughter's killer or killers will be caught, Inspector. Are you sure they're responsible?" Mrs Meredith asked, her voice strained.

"It's all we have at the moment. It's suspicious how the family have up and left the property the very day your daughter's body is discovered."

"Oh my, I can't quite believe what I'm hearing. Not once did she tell us she wasn't happy working there." She gasped and then continued, "You don't suppose they were there, listening to her calls, do you? Ensuring she said the right thing to us?"

Hero nodded. "It seems likely that's what happened. Possibly any calls she made home were done under duress. Perhaps that's why she chose not to ring you recently. Maybe the stress was far too much for her. There's another thing you should be aware of…"

"Go on, we're listening." Mrs Meredith clutched her husband's hand.

"After talking to the neighbours and a group of nannies in the local area who knew her, we discovered that Jacinda had lost weight rapidly over the past few months."

"I don't understand. Are you saying that those beasts were likely starving her?"

"Possibly, or maybe she'd developed some form of eating disorder due to the stress she was under. That's purely speculation on my part."

"Our daughter loved her food. The number of times I heard her slating the girls in her class at school for throwing up in the toilet after they'd eaten. She assured me that she would never be tempted to take such drastic action. She had a cute little figure, there was no need for her to lose any weight. My goodness, what did that couple do to her? How long had she suffered at their hands? I feel so ashamed for not picking up on any of this, I should have. A mother has instincts. I apparently ignored all of mine. I'm mortified about this." She broke down, her sobs tearing at Hero's heartstrings.

He was sure he'd feel the same way in this woman's situation. Parents were supposed to watch over their children, even when they flew the nest. He had all that worry to come in the future. Either that or he could keep them under lock and key for the rest of their lives. "Please don't blame yourself. By the sounds of it, this couple has a lot to answer for. We don't know the ins and outs of what went on in that house, but I intend to find out."

"That's all well and good you saying that, Inspector, but words are cheap. Five days you say you've been searching for this couple and yet you haven't discovered them yet. In my book, that's not good enough."

"Now, Thomas, leave the poor man alone. He's doing his best. It's possible these evil people have covered their tracks well in an attempt not to be found," Mrs Meredith said, sticking up for Hero.

Her husband removed his hand from hers and crossed his arms with a grunt.

"Now that I've visited you, I intend to throw extra personnel into finding the Knoxes."

"You could and should have done it before," Thomas grumbled, earning himself a slap on the thigh from his wife.

"Stop that."

"Don't get me wrong, we haven't neglected our duties in that department, sir. What I should have said is now that you're aware of your daughter's death we can use social media to help find them both."

"Good. Don't let us keep you," Thomas muttered.

"He didn't mean that, Inspector. He's hurting."

"Don't make excuses for me, Cathy, and I did mean it," Mr Meredith corrected his wife.

"Honestly, I understand the mixture of feelings running through you at present, it would be heartless of me not to. You have my assurance that we will catch these people and punish them. If there's nothing else you can tell me, I'll head back to Manchester now." He took a card from his pocket and placed it on the table, at the same time he put his mug on the tray.

"You're travelling back today? Let me fix you some sandwiches or a quick meal before you set off."

Hero smiled, appreciating the offer. "I wouldn't want to put you out. I need to fill up the car. I'll snatch a sandwich at the services, but thank you anyway."

Thomas rose from the arm of the sofa, eager to get rid of Hero, he suspected.

"Thank you for coming all this way to share the news in person, Inspector," Mrs Meredith said. "I know you'll do your best for us. Good luck. Oh, one last question, when will our daughter's body be released? I want to say a final farewell to her," she went on to ask.

Hero swallowed down the acid burning his throat and glanced at Thomas who shook his head. "I'll get the pathologist to ring you personally in the next few days." *Phew, got out of that one nicely.*

At the front door, Thomas Meredith shook Hero's hand and held on to it for longer than anticipated. "Don't let us down. Get these bastards. Fail us, and I won't be held responsible for what I do to them if I go hunting the shits down myself, got that?"

"Sir, that kind of talk isn't going to help anyone. You have my word that we will do our utmost to bring these people to justice. It was a pleasure meeting you. I'll be in touch to give you an update soon."

"Make sure you do."

Hero exited the house without saying another word. He heaved out a large sigh and slipped behind the steering wheel. After pulling away, he contacted the station. "Hi, Julie, I'm on my way back now."

"How did it go?"

"Challenging, as expected. The parents told me that Jacinda came down to Manchester with a boyfriend, a Lenny McDonald. See what you can find out about him. Oh, he's a DJ. I'd like to have a chat with him if he's still in the area."

"I'll get on to it and get back to you. Have a safe trip."

"Thanks, a long and boring drive ahead of me."

He ended the call, put on an upbeat CD to help keep him alert and aimed for the motorway. The first services he spotted, he pulled in, topped up the tank, bought a ham salad sandwich and a sneaky Mars bar and got on the road again.

Julie contacted him almost an hour into his journey. "Okay, he was pretty easy to find. I delayed getting back to you because I wanted to do some background checks on him first."

"Thanks for being so thorough. Give it to me?"

"He's a DJ in one of the larger nightclubs in town, The Rave Palace. Not heard of it myself, thank God."

"I know it. Not visited the joint, but I know people who have. More for youngsters than our age group."

"Charming. I'll ignore that dig. He has a charge sheet to his name, all drug-related incidents. Warned of his future conduct, that sort of thing, never actually convicted of anything major."

"Okay. I suppose drugs go with the night scene, right?"

"Not in my day. Apparently things have changed over the years."

"Do you have an address for him?"

"Yep, it's flat two, number five Cleveland Terrace, Salford."

"Oh, joy of joys, that'll be nice for me. Going from one extreme to the other. I'll pay the guy a visit before returning to base. Any other news for me?"

"Are you sure one of us can't do that for you? It's all quiet around here."

"No, you crack on. Leave this one to me."

"As you wish. See you later."

"Roger that."

Hero leaned back in his seat and stuck to the speed limit all the way back to Manchester. He arrived at Lenny's address at a quarter to five. The door was answered by a young female with bright-red hair and several piercings in her cheeks.

"Hi."

"Hi. Is Lenny home?"

"Ah, he lives upstairs, wrong flat." She closed the door.

Hero pressed the buzzer to the other flat and waited patiently for a response, all the while, peering back over his shoulder to check his car. He hated visiting Salford. He'd had a nasty run-in with a couple of gangs a number of years earlier that still made him shudder.

The door opened, and a dishevelled-looking man hung on the door for support. He peered through the lengthy fringe covering his face and said, "Yeah, man, what do you want?"

"A word, if you don't mind." Hero produced his warrant card and shoved it in the guy's face.

"A copper. What's this about?"

"You want your neighbours to find out?"

"You'd better come in. I'm warning you, the place is a tip. The girlfriend is away at the mo, visiting her folks."

Hero stepped into the tiny hallway and closed the front door using the sleeve of his jacket, unsure what type of diseases lingered in the crap splattered across the paintwork. The sight made him want to retch.

"While the girlfriend's away you veg out, is that it?"

He followed the guy up a flight of stairs. "Housework ain't man's work, is it? Women love fussing over their man, tidying up, that's what they were put on this planet for, right? Well, that and the obvious, if you get my drift?"

Hero puffed out his cheeks at the man's chauvinistic comment. "Not in my house. I do my bit, looking after the kids and tidying up the house. If you're in a partnership, that's kind of expected of you, isn't it?"

"Hey, don't start preaching to me, man. Shell loves fussing over me. If I attempt to clean up, she gives me grief when I put things away in the wrong place. So I don't bother. Why are you here?"

Hero gazed around at the messy flat, sourcing out a decent place to sit. He didn't bother in the end. "I wanted to have a chat with you about Jacinda Meredith."

"Whoa! Now there's a name I haven't heard in a while. How is she?"

"Dead," Hero said, cringing and instantly regretting the way he'd blurted the word out.

"What? No way. Is this some kind of wind-up? Are you pulling my plonker just to get a rise out of me?"

"Nope, I'm serious. I need to know when you saw her last."

He raised his hands and wagged a finger. "I'm not stupid. If you're going to try and pin something on me, I know my rights."

"I'm not. Answer the question."

"Nearly two years ago, when she took on that job working for that family as a nanny. She chose to live-in—that wasn't part of the deal when we came down here," he stated in a rich Scottish accent that Hero hadn't noticed before.

"Why was that? Because you needed someone to tidy up after you in the flat?"

"No. Not at all."

Hero raised an eyebrow at him. "Who are you trying to kid, McDonald?"

"I'm telling the truth. We still went out with each other for a week or two, until she rang me and told me it was over between us. I was suspicious about that, thought she'd taken a fancy to the husband and was bonking him. She was horrified by the suggestion."

"I'm not surprised. Nice of you to be such a caring and understanding boyfriend."

"Hey, I loved that girl. In the end, her priorities lay with the family. She told me they needed her more than they'd expected. To me, it sounded like they'd cottoned on to a good thing. She was nothing more than a slave on a pittance of a wage." He raked a hand through his hair. "How did she die?"

"You don't want to know."

"What? And that's all you're gonna tell me?"

"Yep. No doubt you'll be reading it in the papers soon enough."

"Where then?"

"At the house."

"What house?"

Hero sighed. "The house where she worked."

"Fucking hell. I knew there was something off with that set-up. What did that couple do? Kill her during a kinky sex game or something?"

"Your guess is as good as mine about that particular scenario."

"Gits. I'm being kind when I call them that."

"Did you mention your concerns before she dumped you?"

"All the time. She thought I was crazy. Come the end, so did I.

What's that old saying? Let them go and they'll return, it's something like that. I let her go, but she never came back to me. I waited over a year for her before I moved on with my life and found a new bird."

"Glad to hear it. A guy like you should never live alone apparently. Considering the state this place is in, you'll heed a warning and get down to some serious housework before your 'new bird' returns to the nest."

"Thanks for the insight. I might do something about it. There again, I might not have the time. She's due back in the morning."

Hero raised an eyebrow. "I can see a busy evening ahead of you."

McDonald tutted. "Answer me one question."

"What's that?"

"If you think it's the husband and wife, have you arrested them yet?"

"I wasn't aware I'd told you who we suspect killed her, and no, we haven't made any arrests as yet."

"Why not? You've brought them in for questioning, right?"

"Not yet. We're still trying to trace the couple."

"Bloody hell, they've done a runner?"

"So it would seem. Wait, maybe you can help me out there."

Lenny frowned. "I don't get where this is leading."

"Perhaps Jacinda mentioned if the family went away for the weekend? Maybe stayed at a holiday cottage they owned, something along those lines?"

"Nope, not to me. She didn't work for them long enough for that conversation to come up, I suppose. You think they could be hiding out there until the dust settles, huh?"

"It's a possibility. Okay, if there's nothing else you can think of… All right if I leave you one of my cards, just in case?"

"Sure. I'll have a real good think about things and see what I can come up with. I wouldn't hold my breath, though, if I were you."

"I won't." He grinned and walked back down the stairs and out into the fresh air.

Ten minutes later, he entered the incident room. "Everything all right?" he asked Julie on his way to the vending machine.

"I'm not sure. Oh, it's nothing to do with the case. Your twin dropped by around half an hour ago, looking for you. I explained you wouldn't be long, but she said she was too busy to hang around."

"Why the concern?" He stood by her desk and took a sip of the scalding liquid.

"She seemed worried to me. Granted, I don't really know her that well."

"Okay, that's good enough for me, I'll give her a call." He went into his office and closed the door then fished his mobile out of his pocket. "Cara, everything all right?"

"Not really. I need to see you."

"Is it urgent?"

"I wouldn't have come by your office if it wasn't, Hero."

"Don't snipe at me, it's been a tiring day. I'll be going home soon, do you want to come to the house?"

"Would you mind?"

"Of course not. What about staying for dinner? The kids would love to spend some time with you. They're always asking after their Auntie Cara."

"I miss them, too. Okay, if it's all right with Fay, then it's fine by me."

"It will be. You know she always makes far too much dinner. You'll be doing my waistline a favour if you stay."

Cara laughed half-heartedly. She'd not really been herself since their father had passed. She'd become withdrawn and depressed, although to anyone else she seemed fine. Maybe it was because she was his twin that Hero was able to read her better than anyone else.

"I'll be there around six-thirty then."

"That'll be ideal. See you later, love."

He ended the call and immediately rang Fay. "Hi, darling, Cara's coming round this evening. I invited her for dinner. Did I do the right thing?"

"Hey, you, of course you did. I've made a lasagne, I'm sure it'll stretch to another portion."

"Perfect. Sorry to drop it on you like this."

"Is everything all right? She hasn't visited us in months."

"That's just it, I think something's up. Maybe spending some time with her nieces and nephew is just what's needed to perk her up."

"Give her some space, Hero. Let her ease into the evening before you tackle her about what's troubling her, you hear me?"

"Yes, boss. I'm leaving soon. Helluva rough day here, I've had all I can take. I'll tell you about it when I get home."

"As long as it doesn't involve listening to you going over gruesome details about the case you're working on, I'll be all ears."

"Wuss. No, it doesn't. See you in about thirty minutes. I just need to bring the team up to date on what I've discovered today."

"Excellent, I should have the meal all prepared by then. I've just had a thought, shall I take a cheesecake out of the freezer as it's a special occasion?"

"Cara coming to dinner is a special occasion?"

"You know what I mean."

Hero chuckled. "I know exactly what's going through your head and how much you adore cheesecake."

"I take it that's an affirmative?"

"Yes, although I think the decision had already been made in your head." He hung up and laughed. Fay's obsession with cheesecakes in their different scrummy forms was legendary. Not that he wasn't partial to a slice of the enticing dessert himself.

He joined the rest of his team and went over the information he'd gained during his long day. "That's it in a nutshell. To me, it sounds like Jacinda Meredith was treated more like a slave than a nanny. Cut off from her family and forced to work extended hours in order to survive. Her parents were devastated by the news of her death, as you can imagine. They hadn't heard from Jacinda in months, despite their daughter regularly contacting them over the years."

"And the parents never thought to chase that up?" Julie asked, clearly perplexed. "Would you let things lie if Jacinda was your child and had been out of range for a few months? It doesn't add up to me."

"It is was it is. My take is the mother wanted to venture south to visit Jacinda but her husband put his foot down."

"Bloody cheek. That woman will now be forced to live with that guilt wrapped around her shoulders until her dying day."

"That's true enough. Nothing we can do about that except bring the Knoxes to justice. Maybe that'll go a long way towards erasing some of her guilt. I also dropped in on the ex-boyfriend—a real piece of work, that one. The type who believes a woman's place is either in the kitchen or in the bedroom, nothing in between."

"Ugh…glad I wasn't with you. I would have taken pleasure in putting him right," Julie muttered and kicked out at the desk leg.

"I was grateful for that small mercy, too, I can tell you." Hero smiled at her, earning himself an extra-long glare from his partner.

"So, what you're saying is that poor girl found herself alone, with no form of contact with the outside world by the sound of it," Julie said.

"As heartbreaking as that seems, yes, I believe that to be the truth. Now, does that mean the Knoxes kept the victim locked up?"

Julie shook her head. "Nope, because she came and went freely to pick up the children from playschool."

"Exactly. If that was the case, why didn't she try and run? Are we reading more into this than necessary? It's a puzzling one for sure."

"What if the Knoxes had some form of hold over her?" Foxy interjected.

"As opposed to the obvious, restricting her movements and her contact with the outside world, you mean?" Hero asked, his mind racing.

"What do we know about these people? They're killers, yes? What if they threatened Jacinda that if she either tried to ring her parents, or worse still, thought about absconding, they would travel to Scotland and kill them?"

Hero shrugged. "You might have something there, Foxy. Who knows with this couple? We need to up our game and find them, and soon. The longer they're out there, the more likely they are to search for another nanny and rinse and repeat."

"You think?" Julie asked.

"I think we have to bear that in mind. Let's face it, we've got very little else to go on. Right, it's Saturday, we should call it a day now. I'm knackered, and my day isn't finished yet. Forget I mentioned it, family business."

The team switched off their computers and got ready to leave. Hero left the building with them, and they separated in the car park.

"I've had a thought," Julie said, pausing beside him.

"That's dangerous. Are you sure your tiny mind can cope with working overtime?"

Her eyes narrowed. "If you don't want to hear what my idea is, you only have to say without insulting me in the process."

"Sorry, my way of lightening the load. Tell me."

"First thing Monday morning, I think Foxy and I should go through the archives, see if there are any other possible murdered nanny cases in the area."

"Okay, that's a good idea. I'd be inclined to do a UK-wide search on that, just in case."

"That'll take us ages to complete."

"If a job's worth doing…thanks for volunteering, Julie. Have a good weekend, what's left of it."

"Yeah, right. Same to you," she grumbled, marching towards her car.

Hero chuckled. He'd succeeded in ticking off his partner, as per usual. His day was done now.

*H*ero had been playing with the twins and Louie for twenty minutes, giving Fay the chance to read up on a case to do with work in peace and quiet in the kitchen, when Cara arrived, bang on six-thirty as planned.

The children greeted her excitedly at the door.

"Auntie Cara, come and see what we've been up to since your last visit." Zoe tugged on her arm and led her upstairs to their bedroom.

"Hi, nice to see you. I guess you're going to be busy for the next ten years. Oh, by the way, dinner will be ready soon. Kids, make sure you wash your hands while you're up there," Hero hollered after them.

Cara peered over her shoulder as she climbed the stairs, the twins either side of her. "I won't be long, I hope. Maybe you could come and rescue me soon," she pleaded.

"The smell of dinner will be your salvation, I promise."

Hero went into the kitchen to find Fay with her head in her hands. He stood behind her massaging the knots out of her taut shoulders. "Hey, what's wrong?"

"Nothing, I've screwed up, and the boss is after my blood. I'll need to see where I've gone wrong after dinner."

"Sure. The kids will have to amuse themselves while I talk to Cara."

"No, this can wait. Cara can't."

He kissed Fay on the forehead. "We can try and solve your problem together once the kids are in bed."

"I'll be fine. Don't worry. You look tired enough as it is."

"Border hopping does that to a person. I've been to Scotland and back today on a fact-finding mission and to share the sad news with the victim's family."

"Oh heck, why didn't you say something? That puts all this crap into perspective. Ignore me and my trite tribulations, you've had bigger fish to fry today, and it's not over yet."

"I know, right? Does Cara seem sad to you?"

"I can't quite put my finger on it. Jittery perhaps, anxious. I wouldn't necessarily say she was sad. I guess you won't be able to get to the truth until she opens up after dinner."

"If she opens up." Hero rolled his eyes, experience telling him that sometimes his sister sat on her true feelings rather than airing them openly. It had taken him a good few weeks to finally get out of her that she was being bullied by an instructor at the Police Training College a few years back. He'd pinned the bloke up against his car and threatened him at one point. Maybe that's why she was being so guarded this time. *Bugger, don't tell me one of her superiors is making life difficult for her again.* That's all he needed.

"Sit back and let her instigate the conversation, promise me?" Fay touched his arm, encouraging him to turn her way.

"I promise."

The thundering of tiny feet came down the stairs.

"The herd is gathering." He smiled and kissed Fay on the tip of her nose.

"I'll clear this lot away. Would you lay the table for me?"

"Sure. Either way, I think I'm in for a long night."

The twins barged into the kitchen, pulling Cara with them.

"We're ready for dinner," Zoe announced.

"Oh, are you now? Mummy and I had better get a move on laying the table and dishing up then." Hero winked at his sister.

Cara smiled. "Can I do anything? I feel guilty descending on you like this and not pulling my weight."

"Nonsense. We've got it covered. What do you want to drink with your meal? Are you driving back or staying the night?"

"I'll be driving back." Cara's gaze dropped to the floor.

Hero didn't force the issue. Instead, he crossed the kitchen in search of the cutlery. Fay checked the oven and tasted the peas bubbling on the stove.

"We're good to go, if you are?" Fay said.

"Two minutes and I'll be ready. Cara, there's some orange juice in the fridge, can you deal with that?"

"I sure can."

The children had drifted back into the lounge.

Hero reached out and placed a finger under his sister's chin. "Are you okay?"

Cara's smile was weak, and tears surfaced. "Don't be nice to me, not now, not before dinner."

"Okay, you've got it."

He backed off and shrugged at Fay.

Not long after, the six of them were tucking into the heavenly lasagne, peas and garlic bread. Despite Fay's initial concerns there was plenty to go around for their unexpected visitor. The cheesecake was a welcome treat for all and was demolished within minutes of it being handed out.

Once the adults had cleared up, Fay took the children into the lounge, leaving Hero alone with his sister.

He pulled out two chairs and invited her to sit next to him. Close enough for him to show her reassurance if it was needed. "Did you want another drink?"

"Not for now, maybe a coffee once I have a bit more room."

"Okay, so, tell me, sis, what's troubling you?" He raised a hand. "And before you think about being evasive with the truth, I noticed that bruise on your arm when you reached for the ketchup. Does your visit have anything to do with that?"

"You're a brilliant detective, don't let anyone ever tell you otherwise. Yes, it does. However, that's insignificant in the grand scheme of things."

"What? Do tell!"

Cara shuffled a little in her chair. Finally, she cleared her throat and said, "Mitch and I are having problems."

"You don't say. The type of problems he prefers to sort out using his hands by what I can tell."

"Hero, let me speak. If you start ranting, I'll dig my heels in and clam up. Is that what you want?"

He placed a hand on top of hers. "Of course not, I'll behave. Go on."

He'd seen the warning signs the minute he'd laid eyes on the muscle-bound goon. Mitch wasn't your run-of-the-mill caring boyfriend, eager to please a new girlfriend and her family. No, he was an anger-filled individual. Sure, it went with the territory of being a cage fighter. That aside, Hero had never really taken to the bloke since Cara had started seeing him.

"Mitch is under pressure."

"What's that supposed to mean? Aren't we all? None of us lash out. Sorry, go on."

"You promised. He was the reigning UK champion, and that's in jeopardy now."

"And? Why?"

"He's telling me it's because I'm more demanding of his time than any other girlfriend he's had."

"What a prick. Are you?"

"I don't think so. You know the hours I work. By the time I get home in the evening, he's halfway out the door to meet up with his friends at the gym. He comes home around midnight most nights."

"I knew he was a baddun. Sounds to me like he's just trying to come up with an excuse to finish things. Why did you move in with the cretin?"

Cara's gaze dropped to study her clenched hands in her lap. He hated seeing the stuffing knocked out of her like this. When they'd served in the Territorial Army together, she'd been the strongest woman he'd ever laid eyes on. Now, well, she was a shadow of her former self, and it hurt him to see her spirit so low, just because of a man. To his knowledge, in the relationships he'd had before Fay had come along, he'd never tried to control any of his previous girlfriends. They were free to come and go as they pleased, most of them choosing the latter option when his work had finally interfered in the relationship.

"I don't know. I needed to get away from home. I suppose it was time to give Mum the space to get on with her life after Dad..."

"I can understand that. Blimey, tell me you at least had feelings for the guy before you took the plunge?"

"I thought I loved him. Now, I'm not so sure. I was bereft when Dad died, riddled with grief for months. I came to the conclusion that being around Mum and her devastating grief took its toll on me. Looking back on things, I suppose I was selfish to think that way."

"Why move in with him after only knowing the geezer for a few months, love? That's unheard of. You're usually the most level-headed person I know when it comes to dealing with the complexities of a relationship."

"Maybe I hadn't got over Darren's death as much as I thought I had. Losing him the way I did, well, it tore me to pieces. Maybe I was keen to emulate the love Darren and I shared."

Darren had been intentionally targeted by a madman with a

vendetta against the police. He'd lost his life in the line of duty. Hero was one of the first officers to arrive at the horrendous scene. He still had nightmares about the incident. "Crikey, with a cage fighter? I think your optimism missed by a country mile on that one, love." Hero tried to lighten the mood.

Cara cracked a smile. It didn't last long. "The thing is, I want to leave him but…"

He left it a few seconds for her to find the words she was searching for. When she avoided taking up where she'd left off, he prompted, "But? Are you worried what his reaction is going to be?"

"Yes and no. I don't think he has it in him to really harm me. No, what's troubling me is where I go once I leave his place?"

"That should be the least of your worries. You know there's always a couch for you to rest your head on here. Mum could do with the company as well. The thing is, you don't have to put up with him lashing out." His blood boiled at the thought of his twin sister fearing the man she shared her life with.

"I can't go back to Mum's house, Hero. What else can I do? My wages are crap, until I start climbing the promotional ladder. You remember what it was like to start out, don't you?"

"I do. There's no need for you to be worried about any of that. I've already told you our house is your house. I know it's not an ideal situation when there are three kids living here as well, but hey, they'd love to have their Auntie Cara living with us permanently."

"I know. I appreciate the offer, but I'm getting too old to be shunted around. I need to have roots, somewhere to call my own at my time of life."

"I get that. What I won't allow, Cara, is this moron to lay another finger on you."

"It was a lovers' tiff. He grabbed me by the wrist, let me go again when he realised how rough he'd been. I would never allow a man to beat me up, you know that."

"Glad to hear it. I had my doubts there for a second or two. If the relationship has truly broken down then you need to get out ASAP. Move in here temporarily, until you find your feet."

"What about Fay? Hadn't you better run the idea past her first?"

"She'll be all for it, you know how much she adores you. You're like a sister to her."

"I know. I'd hate to overstep the boundaries, though."

"You won't. Do you want me to have a quiet word with her now?"

"No, leave it until I've gone. I'm not saying I will move in. I'll do my hardest to try and find another alternative."

"But it's good to have an option on standby, right?"

Cara smiled and reached out her hand for him to hold. "You're a special man, Hero. Kind, considerate, compassionate, and a number one twin to boot."

He leaned forward and hugged her, emotional tears misting his tired eyes. "I'm always here for you, you know that, sweetheart. Is there anything else troubling you? How are things going at work?"

"They're fine. Although, I'm getting fed up doing all the mundane tasks around the office. How long does that kind of crap last?"

"It goes with the territory. I'm a DI and I still get mundane tasks filling my day. To outsiders, the role of a copper is a pretty dynamic one. Truth be told, it's eighty percent mundane, ten percent exciting and ten percent satisfying."

Cara laughed. "Don't let the recruitment department hear you say that, they'd be mortified."

"Tough…all right, I might have exaggerated the mundane percentage, but you get my drift. That's what it bloody feels like most days. Take this case my team is working on right now…" He stopped, not wishing to burden her with his problems when she had enough of her own to contend with.

"You were saying?"

"Nothing. It's been a long day. I'll make a coffee and we'll take it through and join the others, yes?"

"You're a good man, Hero Nelson."

"And you're a good woman who deserves the best life can offer you, sis. Never settle for second best. It never works out in the end."

"As I'm finding out. Go on, you go spend some time with your beautiful family, I'll make the coffee and bring it in."

"I won't object to that. First, I need a sisterly hug."

They stood and hugged, a strong embrace that proved how much they meant to each other.

"I'm always here for you, through good times and bad, always remember that, sis."

"I know. You're amazing and a brother to be proud of."

Hero left the kitchen to the sound of the kettle boiling and joined his family. Fay glanced up at him, checking to see if everything was all right. He gave her a reassuring wink and knelt on the floor next to his kids who were playing Mousetrap. "Right, who's winning?"

"I am," Louie replied, a smug grin stretching his lips apart.

"Not for long, buster. Prepare to be annihilated."

Louie shoved Hero away from him. "No way. This is mine for the taking."

"We'll see about that, won't we, girls?"

"Get him, Daddy," Zara urged.

Fay laughed at her family's enthusiasm to outdo each other. "I don't care who wins, just keep the noise down and remember it'll be bath time in half an hour."

The kids all groaned.

"It's okay, Louie will be taking an early bath after I've wiped the floor with him," Hero teased.

"In your dreams, Dad."

Cara emerged from the kitchen with two mugs.

"Here, let me help you with those," Fay said, leaping out of her seat.

"No, I insist. You stay there, I'll ferry them in."

The rest of the evening was filled with merriment. Hero's heart lifted at the sight of his sister having so much fun after showing up utterly depressed and unsure what direction her life was going to take. He'd be there for her, no matter what she decided to do, they all would. Cara was a much-loved member of the family who deserved so much more.

9

On Monday, Hero arrived at work at the same time as Julie was getting out of her car. "Morning, how are we today?"

"Fine. You sound too chirpy for this early hour. Is it going to last?"

Hero sniggered. "Can't you accept my cheerfulness for what it is, Julie? I have a good feeling about what lies ahead of us today."

"I hope your prediction, if you can call it that, comes true. We could sure do with a break in this case."

"Agreed. I've got a few ideas to help hurry things along."

They marched through the entrance and up the stairs to the first floor. "Are you going to share what they are?"

"All in good time, Impatient One."

Julie grumbled under her breath and rushed ahead of him into the incident room.

"First one through the door buys the coffees," he shouted.

Julie gave him the middle finger and then turned to face him, her cheeks redder than a full-blown sunset. "Sorry, I shouldn't have done that."

He laughed. "It's good to have a bit of banter at work, Julie. Do you see me complaining?"

"I still shouldn't have done it, what with you being my superior. I'll buy the coffee. I usually end up doing it in the morning anyway."

"I won't object." He wandered over to his office, poked his head in to see the pile of work awaiting him and retreated quickly. "That can wait." He accepted the steaming drink from his partner and strode over to the whiteboard. He put the cup on the desk beside him, brought the board up to date with the information he'd gathered from the people he'd visited and stood back.

The door swished behind him a number of times; however, his focus remained on the board.

Julie stood next to him several minutes later. "Everyone is here now."

"Sorry, I was miles away. This case has really got to me, much more than any recent case we've investigated."

"It probably brought it home to you, you know, after meeting the parents."

Hero nodded. "I think you're right." He swivelled to face the rest of the team. "Okay, ladies and gents, we need to get cracking on this one now. Up the ante on every angle. I'm determined to catch this family within the next day or two. If that means us pulling in the extra hours then that's the way we should go. I'll get overtime sanctioned if the need arises."

"What are you thinking?" Julie perched on her desk, facing the whiteboard.

"Going along the lines you mentioned on Saturday, I need you and Foxy to research the archives, see if anything shows up about previous nanny murder victims."

Julie and Foxy both nodded.

"I also want us to track down all the people carriers in the area fitting the description of the Knoxes' vehicle. Along with all the known property developers in the area. We're aware of both the Knoxes' careers. Let's try and find out where they worked prior to disappearing. Lance, you get on to Companies House, see how many property developers are listed in the immediate area."

"While we appear to be starting the investigation over again, shouldn't we look into nanny agencies? That is presuming Jacinda was registered with one in the first place. She might not have been, she could have seen an ad in the newspaper. Did you ask her parents?"

"No, you're right, I should have asked the question. Lance, can you do that for me?"

"Rightio, sir."

"Get back to me as soon as you find out anything of interest. In the meantime, I'll be in my office."

His team got their heads down, and he took his half-drunk cup of coffee into the office and closed the door behind him. Before he tackled the onerous chore of daily paperwork, he decided to give his mother a call.

"Hi, Mum, how are you?"

"I'm fine, dear. There's no need for you and your sister to keep checking up on me, I appreciate how busy you both are."

"We care about you. Cara came to dinner on Saturday, did she tell you?"

"No. I haven't spoken to her for a few days. I'm not liking the tone in your voice, son. Anything wrong?"

"Why do you always think there's something wrong when Cara pays a visit?"

"It was a simple question, and you two are part of me, my genes run through you, remember?"

"Okay, you've got me there. I've never been able to pull the wool over your eyes, Mother dearest."

His mum laughed. "Rarely. Once or twice you twins have driven me to distraction with your antics over the years, and as for putting your lives in danger joining the TA, well, the less said about that the better. Anyway, you haven't called me to talk about old times during your busy schedule, so I'm going to take a punt on things not running too smoothly for Cara at present. Would I be correct?"

"Astute as ever. Don't drop me in it, though, Mum, right?"

"I promise that your name will not pop up during any likely conversation we may have in the forthcoming couple of days. I'll test the water, see if she shows any signs of being down before I jump in with both feet. Is she in trouble?"

"Not really. I'm concerned about her relationship, that's all."

"What have I told you about interfering in those over the years, Hero Nelson?"

"I haven't. She came to me for advice. I know that's hard for you to believe, but it happens to be the truth."

His mother went quiet on the other end of the line. He could just make out her breathing.

"Mum, is everything all right?"

"Yes, although I'm hurt your sister has come to you if she's going through problems."

"Don't be upset about it, she didn't want to bother you."

His mother exhaled a large breath, and Hero closed his eyes, knowing full well what was coming next.

"If I've said this a dozen times…you two need to stop handling me with kid gloves. It's been two years since your father's death. I won't lie, some days are worse than others, but you two keeping me out of the loop isn't helping. I need a purpose in this life, and both of you shielding me from the truth isn't helping me one iota."

"I'm sorry, Mum."

"I don't want your apology. All I need from you and your sister is to treat me the way you always have. Come to me to share your problems, instead of steering clear in case you upset me. I'm not as fragile as you think I am. Geez…I raised you two, didn't I? That has never been easy over the years, double the trouble and all that. Your father is no longer with us. All I'm asking is that you two don't cut me out of your lives, I couldn't bear that."

"Oh, Mum, we'd never do that. All we're possibly guilty of is protecting you. If you want, I'll have a word with Cara, see if she'll pop round to see you."

"Now don't you go forcing her hand. She has to want to come and see me herself. Either she wants to share her problems with me or she doesn't. Don't bully her, Hero."

"She could do with speaking to a woman, I think. Fay was keeping the kids occupied during her visit, while we had our chat."

"Is she all right? Cara, I mean?"

"She is. Please don't get yourself tied up in knots about this."

"You can't ring me up and tell me something is wrong with your sister and then expect me not to be worried."

"All right, I screwed up again. I'm going to tell you what she told me; however, I'm swearing you to secrecy, got that?"

"I've got it. Has that goon she's living with hurt her?"

Hero rolled his eyes. He knew there would be no point skirting around the issue once his mother's radar had sourced the right direction. "Yes and no. She confided in me, and I'd prefer to keep that conversation between us, Mum, no offence."

"Plenty taken. I jest, go on. What's the prat done?"

"She wants out of the relationship but is scared to leave when she has nowhere else to go."

"She what? Nowhere else to go, are you serious? I'm rattling around in this large house, and she's telling you that? I need to ring her and point out the error of her ways."

"Mum…you do that now and it'll be blatantly obvious that I've gone behind her back to tell tales. I'd rather her not regard me as a snitch, if it's all the same to you."

"Who cares what she thinks? If she's in imminent danger she should get out of there ASAP and move in with me."

"She assured me she's not in danger, Mum, we have to believe her. What she's more concerned about is returning home at her age. She should be trying to make it in this world under her own steam, not relying on you for handouts."

"Now wait just a minute, who said anything about giving her a handout? All I was suggesting is that her old room is here waiting for her. She knows I'll need to take some rent money off her, that's the way it's always been with you kids. You both had to stand on your own two feet in that respect the second you left higher education. Nothing has changed. I believe every parent should do that for their children, to give them a roof over their heads when needed but at a cost. Let's face it, you don't get anything for free in this world. If more parents treated their kids the same, I think the world would be a better place. Handing everything on a plate to your kids doesn't do them any favours in the long run. Oh dear, I'll let you get a word in now. Sorry for ranting, dear."

Hero laughed. "Hey, I happen to agree with you and I think deep down Cara would, too. Why don't you invite her over for dinner at the weekend, or go shopping together on Saturday, see if she'll open up to you? Then you can broach the subject with her. At the moment, she's telling me she wants to branch out on her own, but her pay is limiting her choices."

"There has to be a compromise to be had somewhere. We'll see what we can come up with. Maybe I could sell the house and set her up with a flat somewhere."

"What? You can't do that, Mum, that's our home."

His mother laughed. "Excuse me. Remind me how often you and your family visit me."

"Ugh, sorry, I shouldn't have blurted that out. It's just that we grew up there, and well…there are memories of Dad in every room."

"That's precisely my point, dear. Maybe the change will help me take control of my life again. I rattle around here on my own with only the memories to keep me company. I need more than that, Hero."

"I'm sorry if we've failed you, Mum."

"You haven't, that's not what I'm saying in the slightest. You both have exceptionally busy lives to lead. In your case you have four other people vying for your time, I accept that. You have to look at it from my point of view. Your father and I were constant companions, and now I have nothing. I'm lonely as sin."

"But how will selling the house alter things?"

"I'm not saying it will. What I'm trying to get across is that I need to try and get on with my life and I don't think that's feasible whilst living here."

"Look, instead of you ringing Cara, why don't you both come to ours for Sunday lunch? We can all have an open discussion about how to possibly overcome the problems you're both dealing with. Are you up for that, Mum?"

"Of course I am. I'd love to spend some time with you all, away from these four walls."

"That's settled then. I'll ring Cara and make the arrangements."

"Hadn't you better run it past Fay first?"

"No. Fay will be rubbing her hands with glee when I tell her. The kids will be so excited to see you as well. Mum…you know you don't need to wait for an invite to come and see us, don't you?"

"Of course I do, love. It's not right for me to invite myself, though, is it?"

"Yes, you have my permission, is that clear?"

"Very well. What time shall I show up on Sunday?"

"Come when you want, we're easy, you know that. Hey, you can make the Yorkshire puddings. Fay will be the first to hold up her hands in defeat on that one. The last time she attempted them they turned out like Frisbees."

"Oh my, I don't think I've ever had a failure. I usually can't get mine out of the oven because they rise so much. I'll bring the ingredients with me."

"There's no need for that."

"You need proper milk, none of this half-fat stuff."

"Okay, if you insist. Crikey, is that the time? I need to get a move on, Mum. We'll see you on Sunday."

"You will, son. Thank you for interrupting your day to ring me."

"No problem. I love you."

"I love you, too."

Hero ended the call and immediately got stuck into the paperwork crying out for his attention. After having his head down for several hours, he was in dire need of more caffeine. He left the office and almost bumped into Julie who was about to enter his room.

"Sorry. By the look of things, I'd say you have some news for me."

"You'd be right in thinking that. I'll have a coffee if you're buying." Julie grinned.

"Anyone else need one?"

The rest of the team all either nodded or said yes. "You'd better give me a hand distributing them."

Julie walked beside him to the vending machine. Hero purchased the coffees and returned to Julie's desk with her.

She picked up her notebook. "As instructed, Foxy and I did some digging into the archives and came up with a similar case."

Hero perched on the desk behind him and sipped his drink. "Go on, I'm listening."

"Three years ago, another nanny was reported missing in the Stockport area."

"Okay, that's within the same area, at a stretch. I'm willing to count it if the intel is good. Tell me more."

"The missing woman was eighteen, Amanda Collins."

"Is she still missing?" Hero asked.

"Yes, she's never been found, either dead or alive."

"Who did she work for?" Hero rubbed the side of his face as he thought.

"A couple under the name of Caroline and Jed Watson."

"What did they say about her going missing?"

Julie chewed on her lip and then said, "Actually, they were the ones who reported her missing. I brought their statement up. They said she went out for the evening with a group of friends and never returned. All her stuff was still at the house, so they reported her as a Miss Pers the following day."

"Have you tried ringing the Watsons?"

"I knew you'd ask that. The line was disconnected. I've got a uniform going round there, on the off-chance the couple are still at the same address."

"Let's see what we can find out about the Watsons while we're waiting. Good work, Julie, this could be the lead we're waiting for."

"I wouldn't hold my breath on that just yet. Leave it with me half an hour or so. I haven't got a good feeling about this one."

"Let's deal in facts, not gut feelings for now. Foxy, see if you can work your magic and find out who this couple is and what their backgrounds are."

"On it now, sir."

"Julie, I need the girl's contact details. Her parents' info. I'll give them a call, see what their take on things is."

Julie jotted down a few details in her notebook, tore out the page and handed it to Hero.

"Thanks, I'll ring them now. Not looking forward to making this call."

Julie shrugged.

"Thanks for the sympathy."

She grinned and tapped on her keyboard as if dismissing him.

Hero returned to the office to find his direct line ringing. "Hero Nelson. Can I help?"

"Hmm…you had to open your mouth, didn't you?"

He cringed and closed his eyes, preparing himself for the onslaught. "Good morning to you, too, Cara. How's your day been so far?"

"Cut the crap. You know why I'm ringing. I've just had Mum on the phone."

"You have? And what's that got to do with me?"

"Idiot. I know you two have spoken behind my back, I'm not stupid."

"You're wrong. Mum rang me not half an hour ago, said she hadn't seen either of us for a while. I felt guilty and asked her over for Sunday lunch. I was going to invite you this evening after I'd finished work. I suppose Mum found it hard to disguise her excitement and I'm guessing she beat me to it and issued an invite."

"Invite? Ha! It was more like an ultimatum than an invite. Are you telling me the truth, Hero?"

"Absolutely. Look, Cara, she's bound to get days when she's down. Both of us are guilty of neglecting her. She's always been good to us. We should go out of our way to repay that kindness."

"Bloody hell, I didn't ring up for a lecture. We're both snowed under with work. Balancing family life is tough."

"Umm…you don't have to tell me that. I have to get on. Be at our house on Sunday, without the goon, he's not on the guest list. It'll be great having us all around the table together."

"The goon is history. I told him I was moving out. All right if I crash at yours for a few days?"

"Yep, the sofa has your name on it. Do you need a hand shifting your stuff?"

"Nope, I can handle it myself. Less chance of you getting caught up in a confrontation with Mitch."

"Take care. The first sign of trouble, give me a bell, okay?"

"Honestly, we sat down like adults and had a conversation last night. He admitted that we jumped into the relationship too soon after his last girlfriend dumped him. I suppose I was guilty of doing the same thing with regard to Darren. He's fine and has accepted we need to go our separate ways."

"Glad to hear it. Don't hesitate to ring me if things change and he gets antsy once the reality sets in."

"You worry too much. Enjoy the rest of your day."

"I doubt it. See you later. Oh, if you get a spare second, can you ring Fay?"

"Bugger off, you can pave the way. It shouldn't be down to me to tell her. You're a cheeky sod at times."

"All right, if I get the chance, I'll do it later. Now sod off, some of us have work to do."

"I'm gone. Thanks, bro."

He ended the call and immediately rang the Collins' number. A woman answered the phone after it had rung a number of times.

"Mrs Collins?"

"Yes, that's right. Who's this?"

"You don't know me. I'm Detective Inspector Nelson from the Greater Manchester Police. Is it convenient to have a chat with you?"

"What? Why? Oh no, don't tell me you've found her?"

"No, I'm sorry. We haven't found your daughter, Amanda, not yet. I'm dealing with a similar case and wondered if you wouldn't mind discussing your daughter's situation with me."

"Another missing person case? Our daughter has been gone for three years now, and we've not heard a thing from the police. Everything dried up after the initial two months."

"I apologise on behalf of my colleagues for not keeping you informed of their progress. The thing is, there is only so much we can do with regard to a person going missing. The statistics show that nine-tenths of the people who go missing do so with the intention of never being found."

"Impossible. Thanks for the insight, but you know nothing about my daughter."

"I know, I'm not saying the statistics are right in your daughter's case, I was just stating facts. I take it your daughter is still missing?"

"That's right."

"Has she ever made contact with you?"

"No. What part of 'she's still missing' didn't you grasp, Inspector?"

Hero gulped. He hated dealing with people over the phone, much preferred to do things in person. Maybe he should have driven over to see her instead. "I apologise. I didn't mean to upset you. Can we start again?"

"Very well. Just because my daughter went missing three years and fifteen days ago, it doesn't mean I never think of her. She's constantly on my mind. I still jump when the phone rings, pray before I answer it, in the hope it will be her, reaching out after all this time. She had no reason to go missing. She was happy in her life. Amanda adored her job and the family she worked for. They were beside themselves when she didn't return home that evening. They packed up her stuff and brought it back to me. Caroline and Jed were so upset, they were both in tears on my doorstep."

"Are you still in touch with the family?"

"No, not at all. They moved home not long after Amanda went missing. Caroline told me she felt guilty and could no longer live in the house, knowing that she wouldn't be returning."

"How did she know that?"

"I don't know."

"Okay, I don't suppose you have a contact number for the Watsons, do you?"

"No. We lost touch."

"Okay, thank you for your help. I'm sorry if I've stirred up emotions you've locked away. I hope Amanda returns home soon." Hero couldn't get off the phone quickly enough.

"Goodbye."

He threw his pen across the room and almost hit Julie who had appeared in the doorway.

"Bad news?"

"I want to see the case file on Amanda Collins. Get it for me ASAP."

Julie tutted and left the room. She returned fifteen minutes later and placed a manila folder on his desk. "Sorry for the delay. I had to track down the file and visit the Missing Persons Department."

"It doesn't matter. Leave me to look through it in peace, if you will?"

Julie slammed the door on her way out. He cursed himself for his abrupt manner.

His frustration had a knack of rearing its head after a few weeks of getting nowhere. He'd apologise to his partner later, once he'd flipped through the file.

Hero sought out the information for the couple Amanda had worked for, the Watsons. He was a property developer which ignited Hero's interest immediately. *This has to have a bearing on our case. Are we dealing with a couple of serial killers here? Did they manage to dispose of Amanda's body? Lord knows they did their very best to get rid of Jacinda's remains. If it hadn't been for their nosy neighbours ringing the brigade, they would have succeeded, too.*

"We need to find this couple, and quickly, before they snare another victim," he muttered to himself.

He continued reading the file then returned to the incident room and called for the team's attention.

"Listen up, folks. After reading through this case, I've discovered a startling similarity to the one we're dealing with. According to her mother, Amanda Collins' body has never been found. She's made no contact with her family over the years, despite them being extremely close."

"Okay. What have you discovered?" Julie asked, her eyes narrowed.

"That Jed Watson was or is a property developer. Okay, this might be a case of me latching on to a coincidence. I'm inclined to think otherwise—at least, my gut isn't seeing it like that. I'm thinking if we track him down, then we'll find our serial killers."

"Whoa! Serial killers? We can't label them as that just yet," Julie butted in to remind him.

"I think you're wrong. For now, I'm willing to take a step back on that and continue the search for this couple. Any news from Companies House yet?"

Lance heaved out a sigh. "According to them, there are twelve people trading in this area as property developers. Here's the thing: I've checked up all the names we've stumbled across so far, and nothing matches."

Hero placed his finger and thumb around his stubbled chin. "Which can only mean one thing: this guy is continuing to go under yet another pseudonym, or his family is."

"What? You think they're repeatedly changing their names? If that's the case, then how in God's name are we going to track the bastards down?" Julie asked, crossing her arms and shaking her head.

"Detective work, partner, pure detective work. You know it'll take us time to piece all the parts together; however, I have every faith in you guys pulling it off. We go over what we know about this family—that's not much, granted, at this point. But it's all we have. Lance, if you can try and track down the names on the list from Companies House, discount them one by one. Visit the people on the list, with caution, if you have to. Once you get down to three possible targets, get back to me and we'll go from there. Above all, guys, we need to keep the faith, think positively and work smarter. There are lives at risk here—keep that fact uppermost in your minds at all times. Where are we with the nanny agencies in the area, Foxy?"

"I've located five so far, that's within thirty miles of Manchester."

"Right, okay, you're going along the right lines. I need you to collaborate with Lance. Give the names he has to the agencies and see where that leads."

"From the full list or do you want me to take a step back until Lance has whittled it down to the three possible names?"

Hero smiled. "Let's go for broke on this one, Foxy. Start with the list as it stands for now. I appreciate how much work is involved in this, team, do your best. Let's get these bastards caught."

10

"I'm off now. I have a full-on day at work. Can I leave you to start the interviews?" Annette applied the final touches to her makeup.

Stewart came up behind her, rested his chin on her shoulder and heaved out a contented sigh. "You know what?"

She swivelled to face him, placed her arms around his waist and gazed lovingly into his eyes. "What's that?"

"I love you more than yesterday."

She kissed him. "You're just an old romantic, aren't you?"

"I am. Okay, I'll do the first round of interviews, but you're going to have to be on hand for the final round. The choice has to be good for both of us, right?"

"Too right. That's a deal. I have one stipulation that stands out, apart from all the others we've discussed over the years."

"What's that?"

"Actually, I have *two*. The first is that the bitch we employ has no family, and the second, that she's outstandingly beautiful."

He laughed. "Your wish is my command. I'll see to the kids today. You shoot off when you're ready. What do you fancy for dinner this evening?"

"Surprise me. What would I do without you by my side?"

"Pass. It's a pleasure to serve you."

"Ditto, although it's you who is doing all the serving these days. We have to employ another nanny soon, we need to get our lives back. The kids have driven me nuts for days now."

"Be fair, they're not that bad, considering they've had to assume another identity."

"About that. Next time, I think we're going to have to consider moving further away."

"But we both love Manchester," he said.

"I know we do. Okay, let's discuss this over a glass of wine tonight, how's that?"

"If that's what you want."

"I'm leaving now. I'll ring you during the day, see how the interviews are going. I'm glad you changed your mind and we're not going down the agency route this time. It's always been a little risky for me."

"I agree. The advert in the paper has provided us with more than enough names to sift through. I'll go through the CVs again, dot all the Is and cross all the Ts before the first candidate arrives. I'm looking forward to the task ahead of me."

"Hey, I recognise that look. No flirting at this stage, you don't want to scare them off. Take things slowly."

"I know. I'm not a novice at this."

"You can come across as overly eager at the prospect of having another plaything in our lives."

"Always fun to pull another person's strings. I miss doing it."

"Patience, dearest."

They shared a kiss so full of passion it left them both panting for breath. Stewart saw her to the door, picking up the two children from the playroom as they passed.

"Now you two be good for your father today. By the time you get home from school, we might have another nanny in place."

"I want Jacundy." May stamped her feet and placed a stray lock of her brunette hair behind her left ear.

Annette got down on her haunches to speak to her daughter. "Now,

May, we've been over this. Jacinda no longer wanted to work for us. She left and told us in no uncertain terms that she wouldn't be returning. You're the reason she left. She told us that you two were very naughty children and that you tried her patience to the maximum."

Tiny tears spilled onto May's rosy cheeks. "We were good children. She loved us. She told us every day, Mummy. I don't know why she said we're naughty, we are not."

"Let's not dwell on that. We need to move forward, precious. Daddy has a lot of interviews to conduct today. Once he's finished, we'll hopefully have a new nanny."

Oscar jumped up and down on the spot. "Yay, I love meeting new people. Daddy, shall I help you?"

"No, son. You can help by keeping out of my hair for the day."

"Aww...I pwomise to be good."

"Nice try, little man." Annette kissed her son and her daughter and left the house.

Stewart waved his wife off then held both his children's hands and returned them to the playroom. "Stay here until it's time to leave, I have things to do in the kitchen."

The children nodded. He closed the door and twisted the key in the lock then raced into the kitchen, filled the dishwasher and ran around with the vacuum.

Ten minutes later, he grabbed the children's coats and wellies and collected them from the playroom. "Come on, you two, it's time for school now."

"Goodie, I love school," May said, her tears for Jacinda forgotten.

"Have you made a lot of friends in your new school?"

"Yes, Daddy, lots and lots. Can we have a party for them all soon?"

"We'll see. Put your foot in."

May balanced on one leg and gripped his shoulder tightly, preventing herself from falling.

"And the other one."

She did the same with the other and then stomped around the room in her bright-red Paddington wellies while he went through the same ritual with her brother.

"There, my, don't you two look fine and dandy in your wellies? I'll grab my coat, and we'll see how many puddles we can find on the way to school."

"I think ten," May shouted.

"I think eleven," Oscar replied, the volume equally as loud.

"We'll have fun spotting them. Are you ready to go?" Stewart hitched on his heavy jacket and shooed May and Oscar out of the front door. He locked it behind him and reached for his children's hands. Together, the three of them set off in search of puddles.

After delivering the children safely, he returned to the house. The first interviewee was due at eleven. That gave him just over two hours to chase up a few loose ends he hadn't managed to get to the day before, concerning three properties he was in the process of developing, which were all at different stages, the first of which was due to complete at the end of the month. He had the final fix of electrics to sort out. He should be onsite really, but their necessity to find a new nanny had to come first. He knew that now that Annette had found another job.

The bell rang at eleven on the dot, interrupting a very important call. He had to promise the contractor he'd ring him back later that day. Stewart made his way to the door, pushing down the anger churning his insides and fixed his most welcoming smile in place.

"Hi, you must be Milly. I'm Stewart Barry, please, do come in."

The petite blonde appeared nervous, her hands tucked into her orange puffa jacket. "Thank you. Isn't the weather dreadful today?"

Boring cow, discussing the bloody weather before any other subject crops up. That's you off the damn list.

He rushed through the interview, his first instincts of the girl proving to be nauseatingly accurate, as usual. He showed her to the door within ten minutes. "Thank you for coming, Miss Jenson. Either my wife or I will be in touch with you soon for a second interview."

"Oh, right. Why's that then?"

"Well, when we employ someone, it has to be a family decision. If the children don't take to you, well, then I'm afraid there's no point in us employing you, is there?"

"Oh, yeah, silly me." She giggled and marched up the drive.

Stewart closed the door and leaned against it. "Give me fucking strength." He wandered into the kitchen, poured himself a coffee from the percolator and returned to his office. The next candidate was due at twelve, leaving him enough time to chase up further trades to keep his schedule on track at the three sites.

He was caught up on another call when the second interviewee arrived. He ended the call, promising the supplier he'd get back to him shortly, and went to answer the door. Standing on the doorstep was a taller girl with striking red hair and very slim. She had bright-green eyes that shone like beacons. He was instantly drawn to her. He widened his smile. "Hi, are you Fiona?"

"I am." She offered her hand for him to shake.

Stewart shook it eagerly. He loved everything about her, even the Irish lilt he picked up on in her voice.

"Don't stand out there, it's a foul day. Here, let me take your coat."

"Thank you. I got caught in a downpour a few minutes ago. Sorry I don't look the best."

"You look…fine to me." He stopped himself from saying *beautiful* just in time. "Can I make you a coffee to warm you up?"

"You're very kind, I'd love one. I've travelled miles to get here. I thought the bus was going to break down at one point. The driver was cursing all the way through the country lanes."

"Gosh, that must have been scary for you. Come through to the kitchen. Are you hungry? I can make you a quick sandwich, if you like."

"I don't eat starchy carbs. I've lost four stone in just over a year."

"Well, you're looking good on it, I must say. Take a seat and tell me how you did that."

He pulled out a chair at the kitchen table, and Fiona sat.

"No carbs, and I cut down on my sugar. I had to do something. Both my parents died from heart attacks. Sorry, that's not quite true, Dad died of a heart attack and Mum died of diabetes. They were both severely overweight."

"I'm so sorry for your loss. I applaud you for having the willpower to try and alter your life."

"It was either that or follow suit and die young, like them. It's been a very sad year for me. Sorry, I made a promise to myself that I wouldn't be maudlin. I've failed."

"Nonsense, stating the facts isn't you being maudlin. Here you are, I take it you don't take sugar?"

"You're very perceptive, for a man. Ouch, sorry, that came out wrong. I didn't mean anything by that, it's just that…"

He chuckled and raised a hand. "There's really no need for you to apologise. Most men I work with have a tendency to switch off now and again."

"Wow, that's a relief. I thought I'd insulted you, screwing up my chances of coming to work here. You have a beautiful house."

"Thank you. We've not lived here very long, we're still in the process of settling in."

"Oh, where did you live before?"

"Down south, in the Bristol area."

"Really, what part? I went to uni there for a few years, until I had to give it up to take care of my parents."

"Umm…near the centre." Stewart had to quickly think on his feet. He didn't have a clue about Bristol, he'd only ever driven through the city once before.

"It's a big city. I was in the centre, too, near the university."

"Did you enjoy it there?"

"Yes, the nightlife was more appealing to me rather than the studying. I couldn't wait to get out of there."

"So, you didn't qualify then?"

"Sadly not. Will that go against me?"

"I don't see why. This position will depend on your interaction with the children and what my wife and I think of you personally. Do you have any siblings?"

She studied her mug on the table. "No, sadly not. Mum was unable to have any more children after me. I love kids, though. I grew up babysitting for our neighbours, that's where my love of caring for children grew from, I suppose. What ages are your two again?"

"Four and five. They can be an absolute handful one day but complete angels another. We wouldn't be without them. I know most parents have regrets on occasions, but we never have. We love them dearly, they're our world."

"I know what you mean. Have you ever noticed the way some people scream at their kids going around the supermarket? It's appalling and mind-boggling to me. It's always the ones who have three or four children in tow. You'd think if they struggled with raising them, they would have had the common sense to have stopped after the first one. Oops, sorry, I shouldn't have said that. Each to their own, right?"

"I understand where you're coming from. It's all about the benefits and what they can get off the government these days, isn't it?"

"I think in some people's cases, yes, that's totally true. I'm so glad that Jeremy Kyle is now off the air."

"May I ask why?" This girl intrigued him. He was eager to learn what was going through that pretty mind of hers.

"I think it was teaching people how to behave and showed them how to fiddle the system. Most of those were living on benefits. Oh gosh, don't get me started on that, I should never have spoken out."

"Nonsense, we're all entitled to our opinion. I happen to agree with you wholeheartedly. I think you're going to fit in with us beautifully."

"What? Are you saying I've got the job?"

He smiled. "We still have to go through the interview, but let's just say, I'm liking what I've seen so far. If the interview goes well and you like the children and they take to you, when could you start?"

"Oh, my goodness, how about in an hour? Here I go again, that reeks of desperation, doesn't it?"

"Not at all. Shall we move into my study? I have the list of questions in there."

Fiona followed him through the hallway into his office which was larger than most people's lounges. "Wow, my dad would have loved this when he was alive."

"Take a seat. Were you close to your father?"

Fiona sat and placed her brown box handbag on the floor by her foot. "Yes, we did everything together, as a family, I mean."

He pulled a tissue from the box on the coffee table behind him and handed it to her to mop up the tears. "I shouldn't have mentioned him, it's obviously still raw for you, after losing both your parents recently."

"Fond memories. I'll be fine. I apologise for not keeping this professional, that wasn't my intention at all. Fire away, I'll answer your questions with honesty and assure you I won't break down again."

He smiled and nodded. "Okay, why don't you start by telling me what experience you have under your belt?"

"Well, as I've already told you, I used to babysit my neighbours' children all the time. I've been on the lookout for a nanny's role for a while now. I tried to sign up with some of the agencies in the area, but they refused to entertain me or put me on their books because of my lack of qualifications. If you'll give me a chance, I promise I'd go the extra mile for you and your family. I'm just grateful to you for giving me this opportunity."

He raised a hand. "Let's not get carried away, nothing is set in stone just yet. What about your extended family, now your parents are no longer with us?"

"I have an aunt living in Eastbourne. I rarely visit her, though. She has enough on her plate raising her four children."

"Have you had much contact with her and the children over the years?"

"You're talking experience, dealing with the kids?"

"Yes, that's right."

"On and off. Let's just say that Aunt Katy has her own special way of dealing with her little ones."

"And what would that be?"

"Give the children what they want, when they want it. There's no discipline in the household at all. In my view, children should be taught the boundaries early on in life. Nothing too severe that they struggle to maintain…I'm sorry, that's not what you asked, I do tend to ramble sometimes."

"It's good that you have a voice of your own. I agree, children shouldn't be allowed to run amuck. Our two are little gems most of the time, however, they do have periodic meltdowns. How would you handle those?"

"I would get down to their level, see what's wrong and decide how things can be resolved without further tears or tantrums. Do the children generally get on well together?"

"Yes, they're very good in that respect."

"Then there shouldn't be an issue. I can't wait to meet them."

Again, he smiled. He liked this girl. She appeared to have all the right attributes for all the family's separate requirements, including Annette's and his needs. She seemed open and trusting with the added bonus that she no longer had any close relatives living nearby. "Just a few minor questions to go now. What about your diet, anything special we should take into consideration there?"

"No. I eat just about everything within reason. Since losing the weight, my diet now consists of regular meals and small portions."

He laughed. "Oh well, at least we'll save on the food bill each week if we offer you the job. No fear of you eating us out of house and home."

She chuckled. "No fear at all."

"What are your cooking skills like? I'm not saying you'll be expected to cook for the kids every night, maybe on the odd occasion when Mrs Barry and I aren't around because of our jobs."

"I'm not bad. I wouldn't say I could lay on a good spread for entertaining purposes, but I can manage to get by. I generally eat far healthier meals these days. I have to get my five a day in. Are the children fussy eaters? So many children are compared to when I was young. I fear most parents have made a rod for their own backs. When I was growing up, my parents ensured I ate properly at all times. I was never allowed to leave the table until I'd finished what was on my plate."

"Do you think that's where your weight problems began?"

She nodded. "I believe so. I tend to go by the eighty-twenty rule now. Eighty percent of the time I stick to my diet and twenty percent includes some treats. I find it works well to maintain my weight."

"Good for you. The children don't have any weight issues as far as I can tell. They eat well most of the time. The odd packet of sweets might pass their lips at the weekend. It's the sugar in our diets that's the killer, so I'm led to believe."

"It is. We've both missed our vocation. We should be nutritionists by the sound of it."

"I wouldn't have the patience for that. I love my career too much to change it now."

"May I ask what you do?"

"I work from home mainly, although I need to travel to various sites during the week as well. I'm a property developer."

"Oh, how interesting. One of my favourite programmes is *Grand Designs*. My father always wanted to build us a family home. He had the plans drawn up ready, but he had trouble finding a good enough plot to fulfil his dreams."

"That's the problem. Every man and his dog wants to build their own home nowadays. I tend to stick with renovating properties. You can pick up a bargain at the auction houses. Annette gives me a tip-off about a property coming up for auction, and I swoop in and grab it. We're a pretty good team."

"How wonderful. I can't wait to meet Mrs Barry. There I go again, being presumptuous. Mum used to say it was my middle name."

"Nothing wrong in that. I've enjoyed our chat today. Are there any questions you want to ask me?"

She pulled a face. "I hate to broach the subject but I was wondering what the salary would be."

"Well, that's on a sliding scale, depending on the successful applicant's experience. As you don't appear to have much, I'm afraid you'd be starting off at the bottom of the ladder; however, as it's a live-in position, the money you earn from us remains in your pocket. You won't have the normal bills to pay if you were renting a flat. How does that sound?"

"Amazing. When can I expect to hear whether I'm successful or not?"

"We'll contact you by the end of tomorrow. I'll be interviewing the others today. Annette and I will sit down and discuss each applicant's merits and get back to you all as soon as we can."

"That's super. Thank you for seeing me today. I hope to hear favourably from you soon."

He showed her to the front door. "I'm sure you will. Take care."

He closed the door and ran into the lounge. Peering from behind the curtain, he watched Fiona walk away from the house, an erection growing in his trousers at the sight of her petite backside wiggling under her tight skirt. "Yes, she's the one. I don't care what the others are like, I've made my decision."

A sinking feeling settled in the pit of his stomach when Fiona turned the corner and disappeared out of view. That alone told him he had to have her.

Another interviewee, a young woman, Joanna Pullman, arrived at the house a short time later. She had oodles of experience, but there was no chemistry between them. He couldn't wait to see the back of her once the interview was complete. That left one more applicant to see before he rang Annette.

The final interviewee was on a par with Fiona, which foxed him. She was pretty, had a good figure and a vast amount of experience dealing with children. However, Coral Wakeman rarely ever smiled, not in his presence anyway. That was the one downside he could see about her. He needed someone around him to brighten his day, in more ways than one. He had a feeling Fiona would tick the box there, unlike Coral.

With the decision made, he rang Annette and told her his findings. "I'm really excited about Fiona. Are you happy to stick with her or do you want me to call back this Coral Wakeman as well, to allow you to make the choice with me?"

"No, we haven't got time for this, Stewart. Go with your gut instinct, I trust your judgement, you know that. Ask her if she has the time to come back this evening. I should be home by five-thirty. I have a relatively easy day, and my new boss is out of town. Can you pick the children up today?"

"Of course. I'm so excited for you to meet her. She seems to be a good all-rounder. I think she was flirting with me a bit, too."

"Good, that's always a positive sign. Why don't you ask her to call at the house around three? You can introduce her to the kids, maybe fix tea together? Or is that pushing the boundaries a tad too much?"

"I'm sure she'd be eager to lend a hand. Shall I invite her to dinner? Being in a relaxed atmosphere will bring out her true character, yes?"

"I think so, that's a fabulous idea. What are you waiting for? Get on to her straight away."

"Yes, ma'am Love you, see you later." He ended the call and settled into his office chair. He swung his feet up on the leather inlaid desk and placed one hand behind his head as he dialled Fiona's number.

"Hello, Fiona speaking."

"Hi, Fiona, this is Stewart Barry, is it convenient to talk?"

"Oh yes, I'm in a coffee shop having a sneaky latte. Can you hear me all right or do you want me to go outside?"

"You're fine where you are. Good news, at least I think it will be. After careful consideration, I've decided that you're the only applicant to go forward to the next round. Therefore, I was wondering how you're fixed for the rest of the day."

"Oh golly, I'm thrilled. You've seriously made my day, no, week, no, wait, my year. Ugh…sorry, I'll shut up now. What did you have in mind?"

"Why don't you tag along with me to collect the children from school? We can give them their tea while we wait for Mrs Barry to come home. She's eager to meet you."

"That sounds great. What time shall I drop by the house?"

"Come around two forty-five, the children finish their day at three."

"Thank you, Mr Barry. You won't regret this."

"I'm sure. See you later."

. . .

Stewart anxiously paced the study, ignoring his mobile when he recognised the number of his foreman from one of the sites. That was unheard of for him. He was filled with trepidation. Another two minutes and she'd be here. *Wait, no, here she is now.* He walked into the hallway and studied himself in the mirror. Not a hair out of place despite him dragging his hands through it for the past half an hour. His heart pounded erratically—that alone proved to him that he'd made the right decision. Fiona was the *one*.

She rang the bell. He waited behind the large oak door until she rang again. Pretending to be out of breath, he answered the door. "Sorry, I was on the phone. Come in, Fiona."

"Thank you. It's lovely to be back."

"Why don't I show you upstairs to the room you'll be staying in if everything works out? I forgot to do that earlier."

She nodded and smiled. He led the way and noticed her taking in all the family photos on display up the stairs.

"You have a very handsome family, sir. The children seem adorable, always with a smile on their faces. It bodes well for the future. I can't wait to get started—if everything goes to plan, that is."

"I'm sure it will, and thank you. I'm extremely proud of my family. Here we go, this room is right next to ours, and the children's rooms are across the hallway. This is the first house in which they've had a room each. Fingers crossed, they seem to have settled down well so far."

"Have you lived here long?"

"A few weeks, that's all. Here's the bathroom, sorry it's not en suite."

Fiona waved a hand in front of her. "That's fine. It's huge. I wasn't expecting something so grand. I am a lucky girl."

"I think we'll be the lucky ones, providing everything works out well later." He glanced at his watch. "Time is marching on. We should go now and pick up the children. I hope you're prepared for this?"

"I am. I can't wait to meet them. I'm so excited to be given this opportunity. Oops, there I go again, jumping the gun."

"Nonsense, your enthusiasm is very charming."

At the school gates, the children ran into Stewart's arms.

"Hello, my name is May, who are you?" His daughter offered her hand to Fiona, no sign of shyness, as usual.

"I'm Fiona. I'm delighted to meet you, May. And you must be Oscar. I've heard such a lot about you." She shook Oscar's hand.

He was a little wary and hid behind his sister a touch. "Hello."

Fiona got down on her haunches and reached out to the lad. Stewart watched the interaction with interest.

"Hello, there's no need to be afraid, Oscar. I'm harmless enough. Have you both had a good day at school?"

"Yes, we drawed houses like Daddy builds," May said enthusiastically.

"That's *drew*, darling, there's no such word as *drawed*," Stewart corrected her.

"Why not, Daddy? I likes the word."

"Come on, you two, let's get you home before it starts raining."

Fiona eyed the sky and nodded her agreement.

"Aww…I wanted to go to the park with our new friend," May whined.

"Another day perhaps. Be good now, and we might have a treat in store for you at home."

The children ran to get in the car. Stewart pressed the key fob to unlock it for them to climb in the back.

Fiona bent down to check the children were fastened in their car seats and then jumped in the passenger seat alongside Stewart. *One big happy family!*

Stewart went to work in the kitchen, preparing two separate meals—fish fingers, chips and peas for the kids, and pork chop, roast potatoes, broccoli and peas for the adults while Fiona got acquainted with the children. He knew everything was going well from the squeals of delight coming from the playroom.

At five-thirty, as promised, Annette walked through the front door, announcing her arrival. The kids ran to meet her. Stewart turned down the pots on the stove and ventured into the hallway.

"Hi, hon. This is Fiona Cummings, the young lady I was telling you about earlier."

Annette welcomed Fiona with a friendly hug. "So pleased to meet you. I hope you accept the job. We're desperate to have someone around who the kids enjoy spending time with."

Stewart tutted. "There you go letting the cat out of the bag. I hadn't told Fiona what we'd decided."

Fiona turned to him, her eyes wide with excitement. "Are you telling me I've got the job?"

"If you'll have us, yes." Stewart smiled.

Fiona grabbed the children's hands and danced around the hallway, much to everyone's amusement. "I can't believe it, I'm going to be your new nanny, children, isn't that exciting?"

May glanced up first at her mother and then at Stewart and said, "Does that mean that Jacundy really isn't coming back?"

Fiona followed the child's gaze, her brow furrowing. "Jacundy? Who's she?"

Stewart kept his smile in place and shrugged. "Our previous nanny. She left to go back to Scotland as her mother was ill."

"I see. That's a shame. Come on, children, let's leave Mummy and Daddy to have a chat. We have some puzzles we need to finish."

Without another word, May and Oscar stepped back into the playroom. Fiona smiled at them and closed the door behind them.

Stewart shook his head, warning his wife not to speak until they were safe in the kitchen.

"That was close. What if she starts asking the children questions about Jacinda?" Annette reached for a glass of red which Stewart had poured moments earlier.

"She won't. That should be the end of it. It's not as if the kids know anything other than what we've told them. Anyway, enough about that slag, she's out of our lives for good. What do you think of Fiona?"

Annette wiggled her eyebrows. "She's sexy as fuck." She sauntered close to him and wrapped an arm around his waist. "You, my dear husband, have the best taste in women."

He kissed her, long and hard. "I chose you, didn't I?"

"You did that. Do you think she'll fit in?"

He pulled away and gazed into her eyes, searching their depths. "Don't you?"

"We'll see. The children appear to love her. I wonder how long it will be before she starts sharing our bed with us."

"Ssh...keep your voice down. I'm sure I'll be able to persuade her to join us before long, maybe a week or two. Until then, you'll have to be satisfied with me turning you on every night."

Annette laughed. "No great hardship there, darling," she purred, running a finger seductively around his lips.

11

Another day dawned, and Hero found himself wondering what lay ahead of him. The week so far had been unproductive for the team, and everyone's spirits were very low. Frustration didn't cover it—it was far worse than that.

He smiled at Fay. She was busy in the kitchen throwing the children's lunchboxes together. He shuffled up behind her and kissed her on the neck. "Good morning, you look as gorgeous as ever."

"Why thank you, kind sir. Now stay out of my way until I've finished this. I'll fix you some breakfast then, if you have time."

"I haven't. I thought I'd grab a bacon buttie from the café down the road. Can I do anything before I leave?"

"Apart from keeping out of my way—this is a well-oiled military operation."

"Well, excuse me." He kissed her again and went over to the table to kiss all the children goodbye. "Have a good day at school, be good for your teachers."

"We're always good, Daddy," Zara replied, tucking into her cereal.

"I'll ring you during the day if I can. See you later," he called over his shoulder.

"Have a good one. Shall we have fish and chips tonight? I have a pretty busy day ahead of me."

"Sounds like a plan. I'd better not have a buttie this morning then."

"Grab some fruit from the bowl in the lounge on your way out."

"Okay." Hero bypassed the lounge. He had to be in the mood for fruit, and his saliva glands were craving the bacon still. He hopped in the car and drove to the café close to the station where most of the other officers hung out at various times during the day. There was already quite a few of them in the queue ahead of him. He thought about pulling rank but decided against the idea at the last moment when he saw the size of some of the men in front of him.

He waited patiently to be served and put his order in five minutes later. That was what he loved about coming here. The staff were super-efficient, aware that most of their trade came from the station. Hero took his sandwich with him to eat at his desk. A satisfying groan filled the room as he took his first bite. Julie appeared in the doorway just as he was about to take the last mouthful.

"Morning, sir. You might want to wipe the ketchup off the side of your mouth before you address the team this morning."

"Thanks for the tip. I feel better now I've eaten. Any news?"

"Nothing has come in overnight."

"As per usual. I'm wondering how much longer we're going to keep coming up with blanks like this. I think we need to get out there and start visiting people again. I prefer to interview people face to face."

"What people? Who did you have in mind?"

"Ex-work colleagues of the wife, the nanny agencies in the area. Anyone and anything in connection to the case. If I spend another frigging day in this office, I think I'm going to go insane."

Julie nodded. "I hear you on that one. I don't think I've ever been so exasperated about a case before. Usually, after a few weeks we have some form of clue to chase up. This one has produced very little so far."

"Maybe we're guilty of not looking in the right places."

She heaved out a sigh. "Or maybe this family is just too damn clever for us."

"Possibly. I'm not prepared to admit that just yet, though. Let me deal with this crap, and we'll get on the road."

"Want me to start making a list of places to visit?"

"Yep, if you would. Have a word with the team for me. I know you'll be going over old ground, but let's see if we can get anywhere with what we have already. Oh, I don't know…you know what I mean."

"Yep, it's as clear as mud. I'll leave you to your boring chores."

Hero spent the next forty-five minutes sorting through the post and paperwork he'd neglected on his desk for the past week. *That'll teach me to do it daily.* After which he left the office. "Are you ready, Julie?"

"I have been for the last twenty minutes."

Hero bit down on his tongue, tempted to make a smug comment to match the look on her face. "Then let's go. Guys, I know it appears we aren't getting anywhere, but bear with it. Dig deeper than you've ever dug before, down to Australia if you have to."

The team seemed more than a little downhearted to him. He'd tried his hardest to keep their spirits up over the last week or so; however, he was running out of motivational sayings.

"It's hard, isn't it?" Julie said as they raced down the stairs to the car.

"What is?"

"This case. How long do we give it before we move on?"

They reached the car. Hero shrugged and shook his head. "I hate being a defeatist, but there's going to come a time when we'll be forced to throw in the towel. I'm surprised the DCI hasn't pulled us off the case yet. It's the meeting with her parents that is driving me. You should have seen how distraught the mother was. I can't let her down."

They slipped into the vehicle.

"I get that, and while my heart goes out to her, there are other crimes we could be solving."

"That's the harsh reality, Julie. Let's see what today brings and then revisit that scenario later. Deal?"

"If we must." She buckled up and leaned her head against the window.

Hero selected first gear and pulled out of the car park. "Where am I heading first?"

"The auction house where Sadie Knox used to work. Want me to put in the address?"

"It would help."

Julie punched the postcode into the satnav and sat back. As usual, general chitchat was absent during the journey which took them a little over fifteen minutes to complete.

The auction house was thriving when they got there. "This doesn't bode well. Maybe we should have checked if there was an auction on today before leaving the station."

"Is that a dig?"

"No, not at all. Simply stating facts. Stop being so damned sensitive. It's getting so I can't open my mouth some days."

"Sorry. Rough night."

"If you're having personal problems, I don't want to know. You know how I feel about your other half. Once a moron, always a moron in my book."

Julie grunted. "Which is why I never talk about him. You can be so…"

He turned to face her. "Let's have it, don't hold back on my account."

"Forget it," Julie replied.

A man in a faded black suit approached them. "Are you here for today's auction? If you follow the corridor down to your right, that's where the bidding is set to take place today."

Hero produced his ID. "Hi, I'm DI Nelson, and this is my partner, DS Shaw. We were hoping to have a word with whoever is in charge around here, if it's not too much trouble?"

"That'd be me. I'm Walter Moore. Today is going to be hectic. I'm willing to give you five minutes, if that will help. May I ask why you're here?"

Hero lowered his voice, aware of the crowd nearby showing an interest in them. "It's concerning a former employee of yours. Is there somewhere private we can chat?"

Mr Moore frowned. "My office is upstairs. There's a spare room at the back; however, it's a little cluttered. Will that suffice?"

"Sounds excellent. Lead the way."

Mr Moore did just that. Once they were behind closed doors, he asked, "Which of my employees has fallen foul of the law, may I ask?"

"Sadie Knox."

"Ah, oh, I'm surprised to hear that. She left us in the lurch a few weeks ago. First time I've ever had a problem with her. She used to be ultra-reliable, efficient in her work ethic. An all- round good egg, until she left me in the shit."

"In what way?"

"One day she was cheerful and happy to be here, and the next she simply didn't show up. I tried calling her, but her phones were no longer available."

Hero's heart sank. "Do you have her numbers? We'll do our best to try and locate her from them."

"I can let you have them later. I don't have the time to sort that out for you now, not with the auction about to get underway. You'll be wasting your time, they're both unobtainable."

"Our boys can still work their magic. Will you ring me as soon as the auction is over?" Hero handed him a card.

"Of course. Is there anything else?"

"Can you tell me anything about the family? Did they have relatives in the area they might be visiting, that sort of thing?"

Mr Moore scratched the side of his face. "Not that I can recall. She never mentioned her parents or anyone else for that matter, apart from her husband and her children. She dotes on the kids. What's she supposed to have done?"

"We're not at liberty to say at present, sir. It's imperative that we make contact with her. Do you think any of her work colleagues could help us out?"

Mr Moore glanced at his watch. "Perhaps. Look, I'm sorry to have to do this, but we pride ourselves on our timekeeping. If I don't start the auction on time, the crowd will cause mayhem."

"I understand. I'll wait for your call. Any idea when that's likely to be?"

"This is an all-day job today. I doubt it'll be before six this evening. Sorry."

"No need for you to apologise, our fault entirely for showing up without an appointment. My mobile number is on there. Give that a ring if you like."

"Thanks." Mr Moore showed them back to the reception area. "I'll be in touch soon."

"Would it be okay if we hung around for a bit?"

"Why not? Are you interested in looking for a property?"

"No, we're settled where we are."

Mr Moore marched off.

"What's your thinking about wanting to stay?" Julie asked.

"Mr Knox is a property developer, isn't he? Would he generally be seen at places like this?"

"I suppose so. He's hardly going to show his face here if his wife's done the dirty on her employers, is he?"

"What about coming in disguise? I think it could be worth our while hanging around for a while."

"Okay, if that's what you want. We haven't got a scoobie what Knox, or whatever he's called now, looks like."

"That's true. Hey, what other options do we have at the moment?"

"We have a list of people to see, agencies et cetera."

"Stop whinging, Julie. I say we should stick around here, see if anything comes to our attention."

"Whatever, you're the boss."

Hero turned and walked away, rolling his eyes up to the rafters in the barn-like property. "I am indeed," he muttered.

Julie stomped after him. They entered the main hall where the auction was taking place and stood off to one side to observe the crowd, most of whom were seated, although there was the odd man lingering around the edge. They had the perfect viewing point, or so Hero presumed. He scanned the crowd once the bidding began, focusing on the men who appeared to be alone, surmising that Knox's wife wouldn't be as brazen to show her face at her former workplace after letting them down.

He elbowed Julie a few times and pointed out a couple of people of interest.

"What do you want to do, talk to them?" she queried.

"No, we'll observe them for now. If anyone leaves the room, tell me."

They casually eyed the proceedings for the next half an hour. In that time, only couples had made any bids on the lots announced. He was aware that Julie was getting restless beside him. He ignored her huffing and puffing, however, and concentrated on the crowd, often peeking from behind his auction catalogue. One man in particular had drawn his attention, a man in his thirties, tall and slim with brunet hair. He appeared to be alone and was standing close to the door at the back.

Moments earlier, Julie had motioned to another man she had her eyes on near the front of the room.

Hero focused on the gentleman who had caught his eye and watched as he raised a hand to bid on a run-down detached house out in the countryside. He appeared to be in competition with another bidder, a rotund man in his fifties, wearing clothes that had seen better days and which were covered in paint and plaster. Hero deduced that he was probably a builder.

He observed the bidding process between the two men. The builder was getting agitated the higher the younger man pushed the bidding. In the end, the builder threw his hand in the air in defeat, and the younger man strode out of the room victoriously.

"I'll be right back."

"Where are you going?" Julie whispered behind him.

Hero ignored his partner's question and lingered by the entrance, peering out at the man. The man gave the girl behind the desk his ID and had a brief conversation with her before she handed him a document to sign. He then walked out of the front door. Hero motioned for

Julie to join him by whistling to gain her attention. He made his way across the room to speak to the woman on reception. Warrant card in hand, he introduced himself and asked to see the paperwork the man had just signed.

"Umm…I'll have to check with Mr Moore about that. I can't go handing out details like that willy-nilly, I'm sorry."

"Call him, quickly. This is an urgent police matter," he urged. Julie joined him. "Go to the door, see if he's driven off yet—discreetly."

"I'm not a bloody new recruit," she mumbled, making her way towards the door.

The receptionist contacted Mr Moore and offered the sheet of paper to Hero to view. He jotted down the man's address and thanked the receptionist. Then he sought out Julie. She pointed to the man sitting in a Ford Galaxy.

"Looks like my instincts were right. Let's go back to the car. Don't make it obvious that we've got our eye on him. He's on the phone from what I can tell. For show, and to avoid him giving us any form of attention, I'm going to place an arm around your shoulder, no offence intended, okay?"

"If you must. You think he's the one?"

"Possibly. Let's observe him for now, follow him if we have to. I've got his address, it's in Prestwich."

"No idea if that's good or bad yet, do we?"

"Nope. Let's go." Hero rested an arm on Julie's shoulder and pretended to chat and laugh with her all the way to the car, which was situated on the opposite side of the car park to Christopher Lewis' vehicle. "Once we're inside, I want you to ring the station, get Foxy to run his plate through the system. Also, give her the address, see if that shows up anywhere."

"What about the man's name? Yet another name change! Want me to check if he's on the list of property developers Lance is going through at the moment?"

"Do that. I have a good feeling about this one."

"The Galaxy fits with the information we have. I can't see that anything else is relevant yet."

"Ever the pessimist. We'll see. Make the call, Julie."

Hero reached into the back seat for an old newspaper and continued to observe the man from behind it.

Julie ended her call and expelled a large breath. "Okay, that was interesting. The plate came back as unidentified…"

"In other words, it's a false one. Why am I not surprised about that?"

"What do we do next?"

"Wait until he makes a move and follow him. What did Lance have to say?"

"You were right, Christopher Lewis is on his list. He hasn't got around to checking him out yet."

"Excellent news. Let's try not to get too excited about this too soon. The last thing we want to do is show our cards and for him to do a runner and start all over again somewhere else."

"He's fired up his engine."

Hero did the same and eased out of the car park as soon as the man had driven a few hundred yards up the road. He remained on his tail, cautious of keeping a vehicle or two between him and the suspect. They followed him to a nice district, all executive-style homes on an estate of around thirty or more houses. "I'm going to park up here."

"For how long? Are we on surveillance?"

He frowned and faced his partner. "Why all the questions?"

"Just wondering when we're likely to get something to eat. My tummy is about to rumble."

"Oh right, I thought something important was afoot." He shook his head, irritated by Julie's blasé attitude to what could be going on here.

"Sorry."

He ignored her apology and lowered himself in his seat to get a better view of the house. "What showed up about the address?"

"Foxy is going to need more time to look into it for me. She should be back to us soon."

"Good. Until then, we'll do a Sydney Youngblood."

"What the hell is that supposed to mean?"

"You know, he had a hit back in the eighties or nineties called *Sit and Wait*."

"That's dredging the bottom of the barrel, even for you."

Another hour of waiting and watching passed, until Foxy finally got back to them.

"Hi, Sally, what have you got for us?" Julie asked, putting the phone on speaker so they could both talk to her if necessary.

"It's a rental property. Took me a while to track down the landlord. He informed me the couple have two children, aged around four and five. They're going under the names of Stewart and Annette Barry. Only started renting the house in the last seven days."

"Brilliant news. I want this couple observed at all times for now. The other car appears to be missing. I'm guessing the wife is out. Maybe she's found another job, it's feasible. You have her name, Foxy. Can you ring the other auction houses in the area, see if they've taken her on in the last week?"

"I'm on it now. Hope to get back to you soon."

"Thanks." Julie ended the call.

"Why haven't you asked for a warrant to be issued yet?"

"Let's take a step back to watch them. As long as we know where they are, what's the harm in waiting a while?"

"It's just not the way I would do it, that's all. I can't see the logic in us waiting."

"And what are the CPS going to ask us? All this is supposition, we have no real evidence this is the couple we're after."

"What's your intention?"

"We'll observe, get some photos of the couple, and anyone else in the house if necessary, and show them to the neighbours of the house where the crime took place. It's the only way we're going to identify them. To me, they're coming across as ultimate professionals."

"Covering their tracks, you mean?"

"Exactly. Let's take our time and jump on them when they least expect it, how's that?"

"And what happens if they kill someone else in the meantime?"

"I doubt they're going to do that, judging by their past record."

"Oh, you think? Presuming they've killed Amanda Collins and she didn't run off in the first place."

"As I said before, our hands are tied as we have no real leads to go on. We don't even know if they've employed another nanny yet. Actually, ring Foxy back, get her to check the agencies in the area, see if either the Barrys' name or Christopher Lewis' name shows up."

Julie nodded and contacted the station again.

"Hi, I was just getting ready to call you back. I thought about that and rang the agencies in the area—there are three in the vicinity. Neither of those names was listed. What I do have for you is a possible hit on Mrs Barry. It would appear that she started working a few days ago at the Hopwood Green Auction house."

Hero narrowed his eyes and nodded. "Everything seems to be slotting into place nicely. Get Lance and Jason over there to keep an eye on her. Let me know when they're in position. Tell them to make contact, and we'll liaise with them directly. Thanks, Foxy."

"Will do, sir. I had another thought, if you want to hear it?"

"Shoot, we're all ears."

"When the agencies drew a blank, I wondered if the couple might have placed an ad in the newspaper for a nanny…"

"And?" Hero sat up, excited at the prospect of yet another piece of the puzzle showing up.

"There was an advert placed at the end of last week. I rang the number to see if the position had been filled—it has."

"Shit! Okay, that throws a different light on things. Well done on using your initiative. Thanks, Foxy."

"Part of the job, sir. Anything else you need me to do?"

"Not right now. We're going to sit here and observe the house for a while. Get Lance to ring me once he's in position."

"That's an affirmative, sir."

Julie ended the call.

Hero punched the air. "Okay, things are moving in the right direction. I'm tempted to ring the CPS but I know what their reaction is going to be."

"So? What next?"

"We need something substantiated, to prove it's them. The only way we can do that is by taking photos of the suspects."

"What about the nanny? If they are serial killers, then she's at risk, and we're not doing anything to help her. That sucks."

Hero let out an exasperated breath. "I know, it's the best we can do right now."

12

A few days before.

Fiona was loving her role as nanny. The couple had treated her well in the few days she'd been working for them. The children were besotted with her, and she with them.

She spent every waking hour with the two little ones. They had made her feel so welcome in their home. Although, Fiona had noticed how May seemed a bit distracted, upset even, when her brother brought up any reference to Jacundy, the former nanny. She tried to ease out of the kids what they thought had happened to her. Something gnarled at her stomach when the kids told her one thing, and Mrs Barry told her another, as to why the nanny no longer worked for them.

On the Friday, she found herself alone in the house. Mrs Barry was at work, Mr Barry had gone off to visit the sites where the renovations were taking place, and the children were at school. She started snooping in the office and soon discovered a file with the agency agreement for a Jacinda Meredith. *Could she be who the children refer to as Jacundy? Maybe that was a nickname she used.*

Fiona rang the agency, enquiring about Jacinda. The woman on the phone refused point blank to answer her questions, declaring she couldn't under the Data Protection Act. This led to Fiona snooping even more. She located documents relating to the cars and a previous house rental agreement in the names of Sadie and Leonard Knox. *Why would they have this agreement if it belonged to someone else?* Things didn't add up. Fiona became nervous the more she dug, and before long she regretted having an enquiring mind.

On the Saturday, Mrs Barry took the children out shopping, leaving Fiona alone in the house with Stewart Barry.

She busied herself, tidying up the playroom for the children. She looked up to find him watching her. "Is there something you need, sir?"

His gaze caused an unwelcome feeling to gnaw at her gut. He stepped into the room and stood within a few inches of her, his smile never quite reaching his eyes. Fiona swallowed. She feared he was either going to strike her, or worse still, kiss her. The atmosphere in the room had become intense and oppressive.

He ran a hand down her cheek. "What a beautiful woman you are."

"Thank you," she stammered, tempted to take a step back but unaware of how that would come across to him.

He took another step forward, his smile fading a little.

Fiona retreated a tiny pace backwards.

His eyes narrowed. He latched on to her hair, twisting it around his hand. "Don't play games with me, girl."

"I'm not. Please, you're hurting me, Mr Barry."

"This is nothing compared to what I have in mind for you."

"Excuse me? What are you talking about? Let me go." She stamped on his foot.

He didn't even flinch.

"We're going to have some fun together, after you've told me why."

"Why what?" Her heart pounded against her ribs, and bile rose in her throat. She was now officially terrified of being alone with this man. She had no idea what he was talking about or what his intentions were.

"Why you've been prying in my office. Who are you?"

"I don't know what you mean, I've done no such thing." In spite of her denial, her cheeks took on a life of their own and heated up under his intense glare, giving her away.

"Bollocks. Don't give me that bullshit."

"I'm not. I'm your new nanny, nothing else."

"Why mess with things in my study? I know exactly how I leave my stuff. I'm anal about the order I put things in, and my personal files have changed position. What is it you were searching for?"

"I swear to you, I haven't touched anything, sir. Maybe your wife was looking for something, have you asked her?"

He appeared to hesitate and backed away a few inches. His grasp didn't relent, though. "I'll speak to her when she returns, but as she hasn't been around much this week, I doubt it was her. Which only leaves you. What is it you're trying to find out? Who are you? The police?"

Fiona laughed, although she soon regretted it. His grasp tightened. Her head ached at the roots.

"No, I'm only a nanny. Okay, it was me. I was inquisitive."

"About what?" he snarled.

"The children always say how much they miss Jacundy. I wanted to learn more about her and thought I would see what you had in your files."

"Why didn't you just ask us? We've told you she's gone back to Scotland to be with her parents. Why don't you believe us?"

"The children seem devastated that she is no longer with you."

"Such is life. They're too young to understand. That didn't give you the right to snoop. Now you have to take your punishment."

"What are you talking about? What punishment?"

"You'll see. You're going to have to get used to the fringe benefits which accompany your position here. Now strip off."

"What? I will *not*."

He slapped her around the face, a hard strike that twisted her head sharply. "You'll do as you're told or suffer the consequences."

"I want to leave. I will not allow you to treat me like this. I have no intention of letting you abuse me."

"Oh, is that right? And where will you go?"

"Anywhere but here."

"You leave this house, and I'll hunt you down…I enjoy the hunt. Amanda Collins would tell you that if she were alive to tell the tale. I hunted her for three days through a dense forest."

"You what? Why? Oh my God, you killed her?" she shouted when the truth behind his words sank in. "Why?" she repeated.

"I get off on seeing you women squirm. Now, if you don't want the same thing to happen to you, I suggest you do as you're told and strip off."

"I won't do it. I'd rather die than let you lay a hand on me like that."

His spare hand grasped her throat. He squeezed tightly until her eyes bulged.

"Please," she pleaded, her voice strained beyond recognition from the pressure. "I'll do what you want."

He released his hold on her throat and her hair and stood back. Arms folded, he watched her remove all her clothes, slowly at first until he tutted and motioned for her to hurry up.

Tears mixed with snot. Fear escalated, and her hands shook as she removed each garment covering her slim body.

"Nice to see there's no flabby skin left behind, considering your weight loss. You must have worked out regularly to prevent that from happening."

"I did. Every day. Please, don't do this. I promise I'll leave the house and never mention what you've told me. I can't do this. I've never been with a man before, I don't know what's expected of me."

"A virgin, eh? Even better. I'll show you, never fear about that. Once you feel my cock inside you, you'll be eager to have me every night. Sadie, I mean, Annette, is eager for you to join us in bed as well. You'll be up for that, won't you?"

"No, please. All I want to do is my job, to care for the children. Don't make me go through this. I hate the thought of having sex outside of marriage."

"An old-fashioned type of girl. There aren't many of you around these days. I'm salivating at the thought of slipping between your legs."

"Don't, I don't want to hear such filth."

"Too bad. You'll experience what a real man can give you." He picked up her clothes, tugged on her hand and led her through to his office. He made room on his desk and forced her to bend over it.

She tried to scream, but he silenced her by ramming a fist into her mouth.

Once he'd raped her, he sent her to her room. She remained sitting on her bed, wedged in the corner, her arms wrapped around her knees, her eyes trained on the door, fearfully wondering if he would demand seconds, until Mrs Barry and the kids came home.

She listened to the joy filling the house and couldn't help wondering how she had ended up here, or how she was ever going to escape.

Her bedroom door eased open, and Annette Barry poked her head into the room. "Hello, dear, are you going to join us? I treated us all to a Subway roll and a chocolate éclair. Do you fancy it?"

The kindness in her voice confused the hell out of Fiona. *Is she aware of how her husband has violated me? Is this another one of their crazy acts? Her pretending nothing has happened and moving on with her life, encouraging me to do the same? Or are they both as warped as each other?*

"I'm not hungry. You go ahead, though. Thank you for thinking of me."

Smiling, Annette sauntered towards her. Fiona resisted the urge to shuffle back more into the corner, not that she would have been able to anyway.

Annette reached out and placed a hand on Fiona's knee. "What's wrong, child?"

"Umm...I'm not feeling well. It came on suddenly while you were out," she lied, her confusion plummeting to yet another level.

Annette sat on the bed close to her, too close. Fiona's body shook, her fear intensifying under the woman's sincere gaze.

"You mustn't fear Stewart, he only has your best interest at heart. Do everything he asks, and I promise you, you won't get hurt."

Tears seeped from Fiona's eyes and gathered speed as they rolled down her flushed cheeks. "I can't. It hurts. He hurt me."

"It was your first time. It gets easier, sweetie. I swear it does. Next time you'll enjoy it, mark my words on that one."

"No, please, I can't do it again. Why? Why do you allow him to do that to women? What's wrong with you?"

Annette exhaled the largest of breaths and turned away to look at the door. Seconds later, her gaze captured Fiona's again, her eyes full of hatred, her lips twisted out of shape with anger. "Because it's what we expect from you. Tonight, once the children are asleep, you will come to our bedroom. If we have to come for you...well, don't make us do that, it'll only make your punishment a thousand times worse."

Fiona widened her eyes. Her heart hammered, and her breathing became erratic. "Please, I'm begging you, let me go. I don't want any of this. I hate what your husband did to me. I never want another man to touch me that way again."

Annette clutched a clump of Fiona's hair and yanked on it. "You'll enjoy it soon, just like the others did before you."

"And what if I don't, will you let me go?"

Annette released her hair and rose to her feet, laughing. "No, you'll never be allowed to leave this house again."

"What? You can't keep me here against my will. What about taking the children to school?"

"You'll be allowed to tend to the children, but nothing else. If you try to escape...well, I wouldn't advise it. We'll prepare you properly tonight, you'll see. Right, if you prefer not to join us now then so be it.

I suggest you rest, get some sleep, because tonight you'll be tending to our needs all through the night."

Fiona gasped and placed a trembling hand over her mouth. "No, please don't," she mumbled behind her hand.

"It's too late. You *belong* to us. You will do what is expected of you or suffer the consequences, just like the others."

"What happened to them? I don't want to be a part of this, please, please, let me go. If you let me leave, I promise never to tell anyone about what has gone on here."

"Too late. You're in our clutches now. We're going to have fun teaching you the way of life, what bosses expect from their employees. You'll join us every night until we get bored of you."

"What then?" she asked, regretting the words as soon as they spilled from her lips.

"You'll see. The trick is not to let us down, and then we won't have to punish you. Do you understand? Don't disappoint us, ever…"

"I won't. I'm sorry for complaining. I'll do what I have to do in order to survive, just don't hurt me. I beg you."

"Good girl, I knew you'd see sense soon enough. Go to sleep now."

Fiona shuffled down beneath the quilt, and Annette kissed her on the temple. After her employer left the room, Fiona buried herself under the covers and sobbed, regretting the day she'd ever picked up the damn newspaper and applied for the job that had stripped her of every inch of self-worth she'd once possessed. She sobbed for what seemed like hours until exhaustion finally took hold and she drifted off to sleep. When she woke, it was already dark outside. She glanced at her clock—it was seven-thirty in the evening. The children would need their baths soon. She had to get up and tend to their needs.

Fiona reached the door and yanked it open.

May saw her and ran the length of the hallway and jumped into her arms. "Are you feeling better now, Fiona?"

"I am, cherub. Time for your bath, is it?"

"Yes. Mummy said she'll do it tonight, to give you a break."

"That was nice of her. Have fun." She placed May back on the floor and walked slowly towards the bathroom.

Annette was testing the water with her elbow. She glanced up and smiled at her. "Are you all right?"

Fiona nodded. "Can I get a sandwich?"

"There's cottage pie and veg in the microwave. You need to eat properly, to keep your strength up. I'll be down shortly."

"Thank you," she murmured and made her way cautiously down the stairs, unaware of where Stewart was possibly lurking.

She let out the breath she'd been holding as soon as she entered the kitchen and saw it was empty.

Before she could move, she felt a hot breath on her neck. Swivelling, she found Stewart standing barely a few inches behind her. She swallowed down the saliva filling her mouth and tried to force a smile. "I'm sorry, I wondered where you were."

"Eat your dinner. You'll need the calories for what Annette and I have planned for you this evening." His whispered words held a sinister warning.

She stumbled backwards, and he followed her, his gaze fixed on her face until she turned and raced across the kitchen to the microwave.

"Do you want me to heat it up for you...the dinner, I mean?"

"No...I can manage...thank you." She twisted the dial to two minutes and watched the timer countdown, aware of him pacing the floor behind her. *Why doesn't he leave me alone? I can't bear this. How will I cope dealing with both of them later?* The microwave pinged, and she jumped, her nerves frayed because of the tension.

She deposited her steaming dinner on the placemat on the kitchen table. He pulled out the chair and tucked it in once she was seated. Then he sat in the chair opposite her, staring at her with every tiny mouthful she took, constantly groaning, as if he imagined her mouth doing exciting things to parts of his anatomy. She felt sick, had no idea how she was managing to keep eating, or how she was preventing her food from reappearing.

She'd barely eaten half her meal when she pushed it away to the middle of the table. "That was huge, I've had enough."

He pushed it back to her. "Finish it or I'll force-feed you. Is that what you want?"

"No, you don't have to do that. I'll eat it." She picked up her fork. Her hand shook, spilling some of the food before it reached her mouth. *Get a grip, girl, you're only going to make matters worse if you falter now.* She determined her inner voice needed to be listened to and bolted down the rest of her meal, even though the food struggled to get past the lump that had appeared in her throat.

"Good girl. See, that wasn't so bad, was it? Now, how about munching on your chocolate éclair? The extra calories will come in handy."

"I couldn't possibly eat anything else."

"Okay, maybe we'll utilise it in the bedroom later."

He wiggled his eyebrows, and her dinner almost resurfaced at the thought of him doing unimaginable things to her with different objects. *Shit! I need to find a way of escaping these bastards, and quickly.*

"What are you thinking?" he asked, tilting his head.

"Nothing. Do you want a coffee?"

"That'll be nice, thank you," he replied as if nothing untoward had ever happened.

She cringed at his Jekyll and Hyde behaviour as she prepared the coffee, any excuse to put some distance between them.

Annette entered the room when they were halfway through their drinks. Fiona leapt out of her seat to get her employer a cup of coffee.

"You're so sweet, a real treasure, isn't she, Stewart?" Annette purred.

"She is that. Are the children asleep now?" her husband asked.

Fiona closed her eyes. She feared hearing the response.

"Oh yes, we have the whole evening ahead of us." Annette rubbed her hands together. "Let the good times begin."

Again, Fiona had to force her dinner down. *Oh God, please, please, strike these fuckers down before they lay another finger on me.*

"Let's get this party started. You two go upstairs. I'll bring the added extras and some wine to help us celebrate our coming together this evening," Stewart said, added cheer in his tone.

Annette winked and chuckled, and Fiona struggled to keep her mouth from hanging open in disgust. She glanced sideways at the knives sitting on the surface in the block and prayed she'd have the strength to choose one to take with her. She failed.

Annette stepped forward and grabbed her hand. "Come on, you, let's jump in the shower together."

Fiona swallowed down the retching sensation threatening to consume her. *I can't do this. Make it stop. How can I ever break free from them? I need to get out of here, soon.*

Annette led the way up the stairs and into the bedroom, where she undressed her. Fiona didn't bother putting up any type of resistance, what was the point?

All the way through the shower, Fiona had her eyes squeezed tightly shut. Annette clearly found her discomfort amusing. Fiona hated herself being manipulated this way, but what other options were open to her? She needed time to consider an escape plan. For now, there was little she could do except to go along with their warped sex games. They went into the bedroom, and Annette instructed her to lay on the bed, naked.

Stewart entered the room with a tray laden with all manner of kitchen equipment along with the chocolate éclair he'd alluded to earlier. Fiona's heart sank. Her body went limp with resignation at the prospect of being the couple's sex slave for the evening.

Three hours later, and her legs felt weak, barely able to carry her back to her own bed. Her torso was full of bruises and her vagina sore from all the implements they'd shoved up her during the sex session. The second she was alone in her room, she glanced down at the tag Stewart had fixed to her ankle. There was no escaping their clutches now, ever.

She glanced out of the window, at the stars glinting in the dark sky. How she wished her god would have spared her humiliation. The truth was, He hadn't. Where did that leave her? The couple had hinted that this was how her life would be from now on. During the day she'd be forced to care for the children, every aspect of their upbringing, from the second they got up to the moment they lay their head on the pillow in the evening. After that, she would be required to endure nights of so-called pleasure with her employers, participating in unspeakable acts that were foreign to her. Stewart had assured her that she would get used to them and enjoy them once the pain subsided and her private parts got used to the penetration. She had severe doubts she'd ever get used to such brutality, even if she lived a hundred years or more.

What was the tag all about? The Barrys had warned her it was to track her movements while she was out with the children. As soon as she veered off course when picking up the kids, an alarm would go off at the house. She soon realised how trapped she was. Any thought of trying to escape either on the way to school or on the way home had been scuppered the moment they had attached the tag. *Crap! How am I going to survive? Will I end up dead, like the others they keep referring to? Is that what happened to them?*

Fiona crossed the room, removed the stained dressing gown the couple had insisted she wore in their presence and studied her battered body in the mirror. She struggled to see through the tears of shame filling her eyes. How had her life come to this? What had she done to deserve this kind of treatment? Nothing, not as far as she could tell. Her parents had always instilled goodness into every aspect of her life, and now to be confronted by such evil, she was lost...unable to overcome the tiredness seeping into her bones. All the fight she'd once possessed had been sucked out of her the minute the couple had invited her, if that was the word, into their bedroom.

Her life was about to end—to her, that much was evident. She had no means of escaping now, not with this debilitating contraption on her ankle. She shook her head in disgust at what she'd become, at the thought of what lay ahead of her, sharing the couple's bed every night as they had promised her—no, warned her.

With no way out as far as she could tell, she flopped into bed. The hours dragged past. Eventually, she drifted off to sleep around four in the morning and jumped when the alarm woke her at six-thirty.

Fiona tumbled out of bed and showered in the bathroom, long before the others surfaced. She put on the bravest face she could muster, pretending nothing had happened the previous day. It was the only way she was going to survive this, wasn't it?

"Good morning, Fiona, what a beautiful day it is today. I hope you slept well." Annette's bright, friendly tone sickened her.

Playing along, the only way she knew how, she replied, mimicking her employer's voice. "Good morning, Mrs Barry, it is indeed the most perfect of days." The whole scene reminded her of an episode of *The Handmaid's Tale*, a series she'd watched with morbid fascination. Maybe acting like the main character in that would help her through this ordeal. It was the only option open to her, wasn't it?

"That's the spirit. May and Oscar should be with us soon."

"I'll see to their breakfast. Can I fix you anything?"

"I fancy some pancakes. Are you up to making some or would you like me to show you how?"

"Would you mind? I've never tried my hand at them before."

Annette rattled around in the kitchen, gathering all the ingredients needed and had the first pancake frying in the pan by the time the children entered the room, with Stewart not far behind them. His gaze met Fiona's. She quickly glanced away to avoid vomiting in the family's presence.

The children were as bubbly as usual first thing. Their company helped Fiona to keep her emotions in check while the couple were close by.

After breakfast, she took May and Oscar to school. Far too scared to hang around at the gate with the other nannies and mothers, she rushed home again, conscious of the tag on her ankle. By the time she returned, Annette had left for the day, leaving her alone in the house with Stewart. Trepidation at what would likely take place if they were in the same room together filled every pore. To her relief, he kept his distance until lunchtime.

"Do you want a sandwich or wrap?" he asked from the doorway.

Fiona was tidying the playroom, lost in thought, and his gentle voice startled her. "Sorry, I didn't see you there."

"It's okay. Do you?"

"I'll skip lunch, thank you. I'm still full from the pancakes I ate earlier."

He smiled and cocked an eyebrow. "An afternoon session could rectify that."

Oh God, no, please keep him away from me. Her cheeks heated up. She ignored his comment, hoping he'd leave her alone. To her astonishment, he did.

During the afternoon, she did her best to avoid coming into any form of contact with him, and spent most of her time upstairs, changing the beds. When it came to stripping off the sheets in the master bedroom, she had to fight hard to retain control of her emotions as images she'd rather forget swamped her mind and she broke out in a cold sweat. *Why did I come here? More to the point, how the hell am I going to break free from this evil couple?* Both questions remained unanswered during her tasks.

With the household chores completed, she found a quiet corner in the lounge to read her magazine for half an hour, then she'd have to leave to pick up the children. If only she was bright enough to come up with an escape plan, or better still, a way of getting herself free from the tag, the one thing preventing her from breaking free from the couple.

She stared out of the window, deep in thought. A hot breath on the back of her neck made her cry out. "Oh gosh, you scared me, Mr Barry, I didn't hear you come in."

He laughed. "Good. You need to be aware that I can, and will, sneak up on you when I choose to. I love playing games with the nanny." He winked at her.

She wanted to shrivel up and die. *Let's face it, no one would miss me. Is that why they gave me the job?*

She placed her magazine on the window seat next to her and stood.

He blocked her path.

"Please, the children will be coming out of school soon. I should get going."

He stepped aside, bowing as she passed. "Your wish is my command. Be sure to come straight back. Remember, I'm monitoring your every movement. One step off course, and I'll jump in the car to hunt you down."

Her shaking hand touched her cheek. "What if the children insist on going to the park, what shall I tell them?"

He laughed, his head tipping backwards. "Use your imagination. Come directly home, don't pass GO, and don't collect two hundred pounds."

The saying confused her. "I don't understand," she mumbled.

"I take it you've never played Monopoly then, child?"

"Ah, no. I don't think I have."

"We'll rectify that. Annette and I will incorporate it into our bedroom games this evening, how's that?"

All she wanted to do was break down and cry at the thought of having to spend another evening in the couple's bedroom. Instead, she gave a brief nod. "I should be going now. I won't be long."

"You'd better not be."

Fiona slipped on her coat and shoes and rushed out of the house, his warning swimming in her head all the way to the school. She arrived early and waited patiently for the children to appear. A few of the other nannies tried to speak to her. She moved away from them, scared that if they were nice to her, she would break down and reveal all.

"Hello, you two. Did you have a good day?"

May hugged her around the waist. "I did. Oscar was naughty, though. He punched a boy."

"Tell tale, you said you wouldn't say anything." Her brother's head dropped, and he kicked out at a stone.

She untangled herself from May and crouched in front of Oscar. "Oh dear. Why did you do it?"

He avoided eye contact, his chin placed firmly against his chest. "I don't know. I said I was sorry to him. Please, don't tell Mummy and Daddy. I pwomise to be good."

"Okay, as long as you promise me it will never happen again."

He nodded. Fiona hugged him, unable to stay angry at the child for long, considering who his parents were and what the child had to put up with at home. *That's wrong. His parents are always kind and considerate to them, it's only me they abuse.*

Fiona shuddered and gripped the children's hands. "Come on, let's go home."

"Aww…I want to go to the park, to play on the swings. Can we, Fiona? Pleeeease?" May whined.

Her heart broke having to deny the child her chance to let off steam, but she was under strict instructions to go straight home. Maybe she could take them the next day.

"Not today. Your father ordered me to bring you home without stopping off today. Anyway, look at those black clouds. I think it's going to bucket down soon. Come on, let's hurry."

13

*H*ero kept his distance behind the young woman when she left the house on foot. He'd instructed Julie to drive his vehicle to keep up with them.

He'd deliberately held back, aware that if he got too close to her—the woman he presumed to be the couple's new nanny—she might freak out. She trotted along the road, scanning the area around her quite a few times before the house was out of view, then she appeared to be much more relaxed as her pace slowed.

To his trained eye, she was agitated about something. He was eager to find out what was going on; however, he'd informed Julie that they'd need to keep all the residents at the house under surveillance for the next few days, at least while they gathered evidence about the couple.

Hero stood, shielded by a large tree trunk, observing the pretty young woman interact with the two children once they'd left the school. The children appeared relaxed and at ease with her, not shy or struggling with their emotions at all, which to him was a good sign. He hated the thought of the children being the victims in this scenario, either from the nanny's point of view, or the parents'.

He was surprised the nanny didn't stop off at the park on the way home. They had passed within a few feet of the play area. If they had, he had it in his mind to make contact with her. Maybe it was a good thing that she hadn't; he needed time to think how to approach without scaring her.

Julie pulled up alongside him, and he jumped in the car once the Barrys' house came into view.

"At least we know where the kids go to school now," Julie noted.

"There is that."

"Did she seem nervous to you on the way there?"

"Very. Shifty I'd call it."

"What are you thinking?"

"That she's under the couple's spell already. I was surprised she didn't stop off at the park with the kids. I thought that was a given for nannies, to keep the kids out of their parents' hair at all times. If he works from home, wouldn't he be ensuring that's what happened every day? To give him the freedom to do his job? Maybe I'm reading too much into it."

"She appeared twitchy to me. Can't we reach out and help her somehow?"

Hero expelled a breath. "I've rattled my brain to think how. If she'd gone to the park, maybe an opportunity would have arisen. We're up shit creek as things stand."

Julie slammed the heel of her hand into the steering wheel. "That's just ludicrous. What if they decide to end her life as well? How can you live with yourself?"

Hero shook his head. "There's no point getting wound up with me about this, Shaw. This has to be all about the timing. Let's look at the facts. As far as we know, Jacinda worked for the couple for around two years. My thinking is that they probably won't do anything drastic with the new nanny yet. It's too soon judging by their past performance."

Julie stared at him, her mouth gaping open, and shook her head. "Your logic is up the swanny. The frigging girl was a nervous wreck in my eyes. If I were in your shoes, which I'm not, I'd get the warrant issued ASAP to prevent what went on with Jacinda happening again."

"All in good time. Stop doubting the way I'm running this case, lady, or you and I are going to fall out, big time."

"Back to the station, or do you want to hang around here at the house?"

"We'll wait here until it's confirmed the wife lives here as well."

"That could be hours yet."

Hero settled down into the passenger seat and closed his eyes. "Wake me up when she arrives."

Julie huffed and puffed beside him. He had to suppress the giggle bubbling in his throat.

Sometime later, Julie nudged him in the ribs. He shot upright and wiped the dribble from the corner of his mouth.

"She's home. Yes, the car matches. I bet the number plate doesn't show up anywhere, though."

Hero nodded. "Okay, here's Lance now. I'll nip and have a chat with him. Why don't you ring Foxy, get her to run the plate for us?" He jumped out of the car and into Lance's. "What type of interaction did she have with her work colleagues?"

"Nothing. They all left together. She was a good few feet away from the others as they made their way to their cars."

"Okay. We clocked the nanny today. Followed her to the local school. She appeared to be very nervous on her way but a little more relaxed once the children were with her. Julie's running the licence plate now. I'm not about to raise my hopes on that one, it's probably a fake."

"Now what, boss?" Lance asked, his gaze fixed on the house.

"Now I'll get on to CPS and plead with them to let me get the court to issue a warrant to arrest the bastards."

"You think they'll go for that? Given what we have on them?"

"The evidence is mounting. Hopefully, if it proves they're both driving around in fake plates, the CPS will think something is afoot and grant it to us."

"Fingers crossed."

"Okay, let's call it a day here." He left the car and rejoined Julie.

She was just ending her call to the station. "As suspected, the plate isn't recognised."

"That's great news. We can work with that going forward. Let's get back to base. I'll have a think overnight how we're going to proceed."

"What about an overnight surveillance on the house?" Julie asked.

He paused and then shook his head. "I don't think it's necessary—at least, I hope it's not."

They drove back to the station in silence, each of them wrapped up in their own thoughts. Hero marched up the stairs and straight into his office. After contemplating the situation, he decided it was time to include the Crown Prosecution Service and rang the department.

At first, they dug their heels in and refused to issue the arrest warrant. It wasn't until Hero emphasised the point that another young woman's life was in immediate danger that they relented and agreed to his request. He hung up and sat back in his chair, relieved. Julie entered the room carrying a much-needed caffeine boost.

"Thanks, you're a mind-reader. I'm coming now. I think we need to recap where we are before we call it a day."

Julie nodded and left the room.

He picked up his cup and followed her. "Okay, here's where we stand. We've got the couple banged to rights as living at the house."

"We still don't know it's them for definite, though, sir, not wishing to sound negative," Julie interjected.

"That's true, that's why I had a hard time trying to persuade the CPS. I managed to do it on the fake plate angle. Why would they be driving around on fake plates if they weren't the Knoxes?"

Foxy raised her hand to speak. Hero smiled, urging her to say what was on her mind.

"I took the liberty of ringing the school. The children joined within the last week. That's another piece slotted into position, sir."

"They all add up at this stage. What we could really do with is matching the DNA of the family to the evidence found at the previous house."

"How do you propose we do that?"

"I'll need to think on that overnight. I'll ring the pathologist, see if he has anything else for us to go on. I'm going to instruct uniform to go back to the previous neighbours, see if they can identify the Barrys from the photos we snapped today. Apart from that, I think we should use the two surveillance teams to keep an eye on the wife and the nanny for the next few days. Let's be honest, we haven't got anything else to go on, have we?"

The team mumbled their agreement. Hero dismissed them and headed back to his office to make one last call.

"Gerrard, can you talk? It's Hero."

"You've caught me at a good time. What can I do for you?"

"I'm chasing up the Meredith case, hoping that you've got something of use for me."

"Such as?"

"Give me a break, Gerrard. I'll take anything you're willing to fling my way at present."

"I learnt today that forensics found a few different fingerprints at the house. Some better than others, but it's a start. Sorry, I've not had the chance to get back to you sooner. Things have been a touch manic around here in the past few days."

"That's okay. I don't suppose you've had a chance to match the prints yet?"

"Nope, you've got that right."

"Would it be possible for you to send me the file?"

"Why?"

Hero blew out a breath. "Okay, I didn't want to go down this route just yet, you're forcing my arm. We believe we might've tracked down the family, except, they're going under different names. In my mind, the only way we're going to get the bastards is through DNA."

"Excellent news. Why do I sense your hesitation?"

"They've employed another nanny. We're monitoring the situation to ensure it doesn't escalate, and I've rung the CPS to issue a warrant."

"Ah, right, so you need the DNA to put the nail in the coffin, so to speak."

"You've got it."

"I'll get the file sent over to you first thing in the morning, if that will help? I'll be tied up for the next few hours carrying out a PM on a child, an infant who was shaken by his mother. Can't say I'm looking forward to getting stuck into that one."

"Shit! That's a tough case to end the day on. Sorry, mate."

"It is what it is. Have a good evening."

"I'll try. Thanks, speak soon."

After hanging up, Hero sat back, his thoughts with Gerrard and the agonising task ahead of his friend.

Ten minutes later, he gave himself a good talking to and printed off the photos of the couple he'd captured on his phone. He left them at the reception desk with instructions of what to do next with the desk sergeant and drove home. He hugged his kids more than usual, the thought of ever laying a finger on them uppermost in his mind. Fay picked up on his melancholy mood and rubbed his back.

"Everything all right, love?"

"It is now I'm home. Have I told you lately how much I love you, and more importantly, our life together?"

"Yes, every day. You're a wonderful husband and father in that respect."

"Good, I'd hate it if I ever let you guys down."

She hugged him tightly.

He rested his chin on her shoulder and whispered, "You and the kids are everything to me. I treasure you all dearly."

Fay leaned back and studied him. She touched his cheek and smiled. "Hey, what's all this about? Has something happened at work?"

"Indirectly. I'll share when the kids have gone to bed."

She kissed him tenderly and walked into the kitchen. Hero hitched off his suit jacket and pushed Sammy, the dog, out of the way to play with his children. Sammy protested and squeezed into the tiny gap beside him.

Hero laughed and scratched his dog's back. "You're a tinker. Five minutes, and I'll take you for a walk."

The five minutes flew past. Sammy reminded him of his promise and nudged his arm. Hero got to his feet, checked how long dinner would be with Fay, and then took Sammy out for a stroll around the block to do his business. He shuddered against the chill of the evening, his thoughts drifting to the young woman he'd followed to the school. Looking upwards, he muttered, "Take care of her this evening." A spot of rain landed on his forehead. "Gee, thanks. Am I supposed to take that as a sign?"

Upping his pace, he and Sammy managed to make it back home before the heavy clouds did their worst.

The rest of the evening went past quickly. Fay had prepared a wonderful dinner consisting of pork casserole, mashed potatoes and vegetables that went down a treat, even though he didn't think he was that hungry. He volunteered to bath the children while she cleared up the kitchen. The girls splashed him continuously, and he ended up far wetter than them come the end.

"That's it, no treats at the weekend for you two."

"Aww…Daddy, that's not fair."

He refused to scowl at them and tweaked their noses instead. "Like that's gonna happen. Come on, munchkins, be good now."

The girls behaved and completed their baths quickly. Louie chose to take a shower in the en suite.

"I'm all done, Dad. I'm going to my room now."

Hero beamed at his son. He was no bother, always thoughtful and considerate about going to his room early, once the girls were in bed, allowing Fay and Hero to share some adult time together downstairs.

"Have you got much homework to do, son?"

Louie rolled his eyes. "Enough. Goodnight, Dad."

"Goodnight, son. I'll pop in later, see if you need a hand with anything."

"It's maths."

"Maybe I won't help after all."

They both sniggered.

He tucked the twins into bed. Their eyes were drooping already, no need for a bedtime story tonight.

Back downstairs, he found Fay snuggled under one of the throws, watching an episode of *Emmerdale*. She made room for him to slot in beside her. They spent the next few hours watching mind-numbing TV programmes, not that he took much notice as his mind refused to shut down about the case.

At nine, he popped back upstairs to check on Louie. He was fast asleep, his books scattered all around him on the bed. Hero checked his homework. He saw the final question had been answered, so he tidied the books away and pulled the quilt up to cover his exhausted son.

He and Fay went to bed at around ten—somewhat early for them. They held each other tightly until they drifted off. The final thought that ran through Hero's mind was how thankful he was to have such a wonderful family, one he'd do just about anything to protect.

14

The following morning, surveillance got underway early. Hero and Julie pitched up outside the Barrys' home, while Lance and Jason showed up at Mrs Barry's place of employment. It turned out to be an exceptionally long day. Neither the nanny nor Mr Barry left the house until mid-afternoon.

"Finally! To say I was losing the will to live would be a bloody understatement." Hero started the engine and crawled along behind the nanny. He couldn't help noticing that she was just as nervous as she'd seemed the previous day.

"Are you going to try to speak to her today?" Julie asked.

"If I can. It's a dry day. Maybe she'll stop off at the park on the way home."

"Here's hoping. I can't see how we're supposed to help out if she doesn't. There's no telling how long those damn warrants are going to take. Every extra hour she's alone in the house with the Barrys, is another hour off her life."

"Don't say that. I feel guilty enough about leaving her in that damned house as it is."

"So do I. A necessary risk until the CPS get their act together."

The nanny stopped outside the school. She stood alone, away from all the other mothers or nannies waiting to collect their children. Hero's heart went out to the poor girl, who looked lost and bewildered. He wished he could jump in there and save her from what she was having to endure. His hands were blasted well tied on that one.

He and Julie watched the children run up to her, showing off the cardboard cut-outs of some animals they'd created during the day. Together, the three of them headed back to the house, the children both animated beside her.

"Please, go into the park," Hero muttered as the entrance loomed closer.

"Why is she looking around her? Do you think she suspects we're watching her?"

Hero shrugged. Julie had a good point. If only he could read the nanny's mind, this whole debacle could be brought to a halt instantly. "Yes, she's going in."

"Crap, this is our chance."

Hero turned to Julie. "It could be the only one we get, let's not mess it up."

They held back for a few moments to give the kids time to get settled on the equipment. They ran between the various apparatus, calling out to the nanny, whom Hero picked up as being called Fiona, to watch them.

Hero's heart rate sped up, and he walked towards the woman. Julie took a wide circle and approached from the rear.

"Hello, Fiona. Please, don't be alarmed, we're the police."

"No. Don't come near me, I'm begging you."

"Keep calm. Don't let the children suspect anything. We're here to help you."

"You know?" She faced Hero, tears bulging in her green, panic-stricken eyes.

"We do. We're doing everything we can to help you. Do you have it in you to continue as you are, without alerting the family?"

"I think so. Please, they hurt me. You have to get me out of there."

"Okay, bear with us. We're arranging to get arrest warrants for the couple now."

What she said next in a whisper tore him apart. "They do things to me...every night. I *have* no escape. I shouldn't be here now. The children pleaded with me to bring them here." She glanced down at her legs and pulled up her trousers to reveal an ankle tag.

"Shit! They're monitoring your every move."

Fiona nodded. "They've warned me that if I try to escape, they'll hunt me down and kill me. They've done it before to an Amanda Collins."

"Damn. Okay, you need to trust us. Go back to the house with the children. Don't raise their suspicions. Can you do that?"

"Oh God, do I have to? Can't you arrest them now?"

"Unfortunately, our hands are tied for now. I promise, I'll do my best to try to hurry things along. I need you to remain calm and go about your usual business. If either of them cottons on to our presence, well, they could take off and start over again."

"They're killers. How do you propose I act around them? I can't sleep. I'm living in constant fear." She scanned the park for the children and gasped. "Shit! He's here. Go away, leave me alone." She scurried across the park to find the children.

Mr Barry glared at her as she strode towards him.

"Fuck, he looks angry. I hope we haven't made matters worse for her." Hero walked back to the car with Julie, desperately trying not to glance over his shoulder to see the man's reaction to the nanny. Inside the car, he expelled a large breath. "I'm going to hound the bloody CPS until they issue those frigging warrants. That poor girl's life is in jeopardy. They need to shift their arses and help us get her out of there."

"I agree. She's petrified and living under constant threat. You could mention what she said about Amanda and the fact they 'make her do things', plus they have a tag on her. That should help."

Hero dialled the CPS and pleaded with the person he connected with to escalate his request. They assured him that he was in the queue and that he should hear back from them soon.

"I'm not being melodramatic here, but this nanny is in grave danger. She's admitted to me that the couple are doing things to her daily. To me that sounds like they're raping her. Plus, they've attached a tag to her leg. I need to get this girl out of there, pronto. Tomorrow could be too late. She could be dead by then. We also have reason to believe the couple killed a previous nanny, a girl who was reported missing."

"Okay, leave it with me. I'll see what I can do," the man on the other end assured him.

"Thanks. There isn't much time left to serve the warrant today, please hurry." He ended the call.

All the time he was pleading with the CPS, his gaze was trained on Fiona and the man they knew as Stewart Barry. He detested the way he was glaring at the nanny and suspected she would feel the man's wrath once they were behind closed doors.

"You're fearing for her safety now, aren't you?" Julie asked astutely.

"Aren't you? Shit, fuck procedures, we need to help that girl before it's too fucking late. You know what? I hate this job at times like this."

"There's no point in you getting worked up about something we can't change. You've done your best."

"Which obviously isn't good enough." He slammed his fist against his thigh. It jarred his wrist and forearm. The pain gave him something else to think about for a few seconds instead of the young woman's plight.

They watched Barry, Fiona and the two children leave the park ten minutes later. Hero decided to remain where he was in case Barry got suspicious of them following them back to the house.

When he thought the coast was clear, Hero drove back to the house and tucked the car behind a van in a nearby road that gave them access to view a snippet of the home.

"What now?"

"We wait it out, all the time cursing the CPS for dragging their damn heels."

His mobile rang. He answered it immediately, thinking it would be the call he was waiting for. It wasn't. It turned out to be Lance, informing him that Mrs Barry had left work early and appeared to be on her way back to the house.

"Right, get over here, Lance. I'll fill you in on what's gone on when you arrive." He threw his mobile on the dashboard. "That doesn't bode well. I'm sensing we've put her more at risk than she was in the first place. Why the fuck did I speak to her? Why?"

"No recriminations. We don't know that's the case. Mrs Barry could have a dentist appointment or something along those lines, we don't know for sure."

"You're right. Damn, where are those frigging warrants? It's coming up to five now and still no sign of them."

Mrs Barry's car turned into the drive. She rushed through the front door, which only added to Hero's anxiety.

"Are you up for some overtime? I really don't want to leave here tonight, not with Fiona in jeopardy."

"I was about to suggest the same. There's a shop on the corner. Want me to grab a few snacks?"

Hero removed a twenty from his wallet. "Thanks, Julie. Get something for Jason and Lance, too, if you would."

"Twenty won't cover it, I'll add to it." She jumped out of the car before he could offer her any more money.

Lance pulled into a space on the opposite side of the road. He and Jason jumped in the back of Hero's car, and he brought them up to speed on what had happened at the park.

"Shit! That sounds ominous, guv, are you sure there's no way around this? The girl's life is in danger. Surely that has to count for something."

"It doesn't. If I go against the CPS, I might as well kiss my career goodbye, guys. Believe me when I tell you this situation is the pits for me."

Julie reappeared with a veritable feast of sandwiches and pork pies, and cans of Coke to wash it all down with.

The four of them agreed to remain on surveillance during the course of the night. They took it in turns to have a nap. There was no way Hero would leave there tonight, not with Fiona in danger.

The lights went on in the house, downstairs first and then upstairs as the family got ready for the evening.

At eight-thirty, Hero nudged Julie awake. "What do you make of that?"

Julie strained her tired eyes at the house. "I'm not with you."

"The light is flashing on and off in the bedroom on the right."

"Ah, I see it. Holy shit!"

"What is it?"

"Could it be Morse code? Either way, it looks like someone is sending an SOS message."

"Oh fuck! Okay, I'm going in. I can't hold back another moment. That girl is bloody desperate for our help."

Julie grabbed his forearm as he flung the driver's door open. "Be careful."

"Of course. Let Jason and Lance know what's happening; tell one of them to join me. You stay here, watch the proceedings if you can, be ready to call for backup if it's needed."

"I've got your back, sir."

Hero crouched as he crossed the road. Sticking to the edge of the garden, aware there was a motion sensor light above the front door, he rounded the garden.

Lance whispered behind him, "I'm here, sir. What's your plan?"

"To get her out of there."

"What? How?"

"Damn, why do you insist on asking such dumb questions, man, as if I've figured that frigging part out yet? Just follow my lead. She's there, standing at the window, pleading with us to help her. I can't bloody ignore that."

Lance nodded. "I agree. We have to rescue her."

They continued the rest of their journey. Hero's legs were already aching because of his stance. He shook them out and darted the final part to stand beneath the window where Fiona was standing. He gestured for her to open the window if she could. It was a relief to see her peer out at them. "Can you jump?"

"No, I have a fear of heights," she whispered back.

"You're going to have to overcome that fear. I'll catch you."

"I can't. They're next door, they might hear me."

"We need to get you out of there. Jump, Fiona. I can't protect you otherwise. You have to leave the house under your own steam."

She hesitated for what seemed to be an eternity. Finally, she emerged and perched on the windowsill.

"Lance, get ready to catch her with me."

The two of them linked hands.

"Okay, jump, Fiona. Don't think about it, just do it."

The next moment, he and Lance braced themselves, ready to break her fall.

Fiona sobbed. Her hand was pressed over her mouth in an attempt not to cry out. Hero and Lance retraced their steps back around the garden, with Fiona between them. Once they got to the road, Hero glanced back at the house. All was as it should be. He placed Fiona in the back of his car and instructed Lance and Jason to take over the surveillance while he and Julie whisked Fiona off to hospital.

"I don't want to go to hospital, please, I just need to go somewhere safe, where they can't find me."

"You're safe with us. Did anything happen tonight?"

"No, they threatened they would come for me at ten o'clock."

"And do what?" Hero asked, peering sideways at his partner as he drove.

"They didn't tell me. I can imagine it wouldn't be pleasant. He punished me, hit me a few times once the children were out of the way when we got back to the house."

"Because you spoke to me?"

"Yes. I told him you were after a nanny and asking my advice where to look for one, but he didn't believe me. I've been scared shitless all afternoon. She came home early and laid into me with her fists, too. I couldn't stand it any longer."

"I regret making the situation more dangerous for you. They can't hurt you any more, Fiona."

"What if he tracks me down? The tag! He said he would hunt me, punish me, if ever I tried to escape. What about the children? They're still in the house with those monsters. I can't bear the thought of leaving them alone with them. They're not safe, they can't be."

"To your knowledge, have they ever laid a hand on the kids?" he asked, watching her reaction in his rear-view mirror.

"No, I don't think so."

"Then that's not your concern. Let's get you checked over at the hospital and worry about the rest of it later."

She nodded, and tears tumbled down her cheeks. "Thank you, for saving me." She laid down on the back seat.

Hero swallowed down the lump in his throat.

They arrived at the hospital. Before they entered, Hero took out a set of bolt cutters from his boot and snipped off the tag. Entering the main building, they made their way to the Accident and Emergency Department where the doctors and nurses cared for her with kid gloves once Hero had made them aware of the situation. They insisted she should be admitted for observation overnight. Hero was grateful for small mercies and rang the station to instruct the desk sergeant to appoint a uniformed officer to guard her room.

Then Hero and Julie called it a night. He checked in on Lance and Jason before he switched off the light and went to sleep. The men assured him, as far as they could tell, all was quiet at the house.

He was woken up at two-fifteen by his mobile vibrating under his pillow. Fay stirred beside him and groaned her displeasure. "Shit, sorry, love." He shot out of bed and took the call in the bathroom. "Lance, what's wrong?"

"Guv, they're on the move. The whole family is in the people carrier. We're following them and have called for backup."

"Fuck. Okay. I'll get dressed and join you. Do not let them out of your sight."

"That's a given, sir. Let me know when you're mobile and I'll send you our location."

"Good man. I'll be five minutes." He hurriedly slipped into a pair of jeans, T-shirt and jumper. He then pecked Fay on the forehead and briefly explained the situation to her. She was semi-comatose, and he doubted if she'd remember what he said in the morning so wrote a brief note and left it on the kitchen table. He ruffled Sammy's head and rushed out of the house.

He contacted Lance who gave him the location, which was around fifteen minutes away from his home. He drove like a man on a mission. Lance updated his position regularly and assured Hero that backup was imminent.

"Use a stinger on them. Do *not* let them get away, you hear me? I'm two minutes from you, coming in from the opposite direction. Let's get the bastards. Make sure the other officers are aware that there are two kids on board."

"They're already aware of that, sir."

Hero put the pedal to the metal, grateful there weren't many vehicles on the road at this ungodly hour of the morning.

He rounded the next corner and almost crashed into a Ford Galaxy coming towards him, driving erratically. He ended up mounting the kerb in his attempt to avoid a collision. Lance's car flew past him, along with two patrol cars. Hero yanked on the steering wheel and joined the convoy. Around a mile or so up the road, the cars all came to a standstill, once the stinger trap had been deployed.

Hero jumped out and stormed towards the car. One of the uniformed officers was shouting at the Barrys to get out of the vehicle. He had a Taser trained on Stewart Barry whose expression was one of resignation.

Lance ran forward, opened the passenger door and encouraged Annette Barry to step out. She lunged at him, her nails slashing at his face until Jason pulled her off.

"Cuff her," Hero instructed, glaring at the woman.

She laughed and spat at his feet.

"Nice way to act in front of your children, I must say," Hero stated, narrowing his eyes. "Jason, put the kids in the back of my car. I'll personally see to it that Social Services find a decent family to bring them up. I'm guessing it'll be a change for them to be in a stable, loving environment."

"Leave my kids alone. They're going nowhere," Annette Barry shouted, wrestling to get free of Lance.

Hero shook his head. "Get her out of my sight." He turned his attention to Stewart Barry. "What about you? Haven't you got anything to say?"

"I'll have my day in court. Until then, I'm saying nothing. What are the words? Oh yeah, *no comment*."

"You can go down that route if you like, it's no skin off my nose, Barry or whatever your real name is. We have indisputable DNA evidence that will bang you up for years. Oh yes, and this time round, we have a living witness that will ensure you and your twisted wife spend the rest of your time in prison."

Barry shrugged. "Whatever. We'll soon see who comes out on top."

"Take him to the station. Throw them both in the cells. I'll interview them in the morning."

"Okay, boss." Jason led the cuffed killer to his vehicle, and Lance placed the venomous-mouthed Annette Barry in the back of one of the attending patrol cars.

During the journey to the station, Hero tried to hold a conversation with the two children, trying his utmost to reassure them everything would be all right. He'd rung ahead, asked the desk sergeant to put in a call to the emergency Social Services number and was pleased to see a woman from Social Services already at the station when he arrived. He handed the children over and signed the necessary paperwork she had with her.

"Take care of them, they're shaken up. Who knows what trauma they've been subjected to over the years?"

"I want my mummy and daddy," the little girl asked.

Hero got down on his haunches and held her hand. "What's your name, sweetheart?"

Pitiful tears brimming her eyes, she shrugged. "I don't know any more."

"That's okay. Don't be scared. You and your brother will be cared for properly from now on. Go with this lady, she'll find you a nice family to stay with for now." He cupped her cheek with his hand, and her tears finally flowed. He stood and said to the woman, "Can you leave now? The others are due back anytime soon."

The woman from Social Services nodded and steered the children out of the building and into her car, a female officer by her side in case either of the children decided to make a run for it. Although, Hero felt the little ones were far too traumatised to try to do anything foolish. He hung around until he knew the mother and father were safely banged up, then he drove home, eager to get back to his 'normal family'.

EPILOGUE

*E*xhausted, Hero conducted the interviews with the Barrys the following day. They both refused to openly admit their guilt. In the grand scheme of things, he knew if they insisted on remaining quiet, it would only go against them. He had them bang to rights. The DNA from the house where they'd found Jacinda Meredith's body, plus the confirmation from the neighbours they were the Knoxes, would be their undoing—that and the fact the couple had created new personas for themselves and were driving around with fake plates. As it was, they didn't need the arrest warrants, even though the CPS finally gave them the go-ahead that morning to arrest the couple—ten hours too late!

Hero visited Fiona in hospital that afternoon. She was on tenterhooks, but her relief was evident in the way she broke down in his arms the moment he confirmed that the Barrys had been arrested and were sitting in a cell awaiting to be transferred to the remand centre.

He congratulated his team on yet another case solved. They celebrated down at the pub after work that evening. Hero stopped off for a swift pint but put thirty quid behind the bar for the others to get tipsy on. They deserved it.

The rest of the week consisted of mind-numbing paperwork for all the team. Come six o'clock on Friday, Hero was totally ready for the weekend, and so was his team.

Saturday was spent shopping and generally having a good time with the kids. They were all looking forward to Grandma and Auntie Cara coming for Sunday lunch.

On Sunday, everything was ready early. Fay and Hero had worked well together to prepare all the vegetables, and by the time the beef was half-cooked, his mother and sister arrived.

The kids excitedly greeted them at the front door, relieving them of the goodie bags they'd brought for them. Hero smiled. Having all his family around him finally put life back into perspective, even though there was a crucial family member missing. He sensed his father wasn't far, watching over them.

It was a truly memorable day. Under their grandmother's adoring gaze, the kids played with the games she'd bought them. Around five o'clock, Hero announced that he was taking Sammy for a walk. To his disbelief, everyone volunteered to go with him.

Once they were back home, talk of food resurfaced. The adults all helped to prepare a light tea in the kitchen. It was after this was eaten and out of the way that Hero's mother drew everyone's attention.

"I have an announcement to make and I'd prefer it if you allowed me to finish what I want to say without any interruptions." Her words were mostly directed at Hero.

He frowned. Without realising what he was doing, he reached for Fay's hand. "Sounds ominous, Mother."

"Hush now. Okay, I've been considering this for a few months now, and providing Hero doesn't object, I intend to sell the house and split the proceeds with Cara. He can have his half of my estate once I'm gone."

"What? No, Mum, you can't do that," Cara shouted, appearing stunned.

"I can, and I will. You need to get a foot on the property ladder. I'm rambling around a large house which is full of memories... Hero, what do you have to say on the matter?"

He released Fay's hand and crossed the room to where his mother was standing. He held out a hand to Cara and drew her closer, then he placed an arm around his mother's shoulder and kissed her on the head. "I think it's a fabulous idea. Dad would be proud of you, Mum."

His mother's shoulders sagged, and she blew out the breath she'd been holding in. "I'm so relieved. Are you sure you don't mind?"

He hugged her. "Of course I'm sure. It seems an ideal solution for both of you. What do you think, Cara?"

"I'm gobsmacked, Mum. Are you sure?"

"Of course I am, love. It'll come to you eventually anyway. Why not make use of the money now when you need it the most? We could go house hunting together. I've got my eye on a neat little bungalow on a new development not far from here."

"Sounds fantastic. It'll be lovely to have you close by, Mum," Hero said, his smile broadening.

"I could take a look there, too, it makes sense. I can't thank you enough for this, Mum. You have my word I won't waste the money."

Their mother sniggered. "I think you'd be in bother with Hero if you did."

"Too right. Okay, let's open a bottle of wine to celebrate."

Fay prepared wine for the adults and orange juice for the children. They chinked their glasses together.

"To family," Hero toasted.

THE END

NOTE TO THE READER

Dear Reader,

What a heart-wrenching read that was.

But as usual, Hero and his team came to the rescue in his own inimitable way. A gruesome tale never the less, I'm sure you'll agree.

Look out for more from Hero Nelson during 2020

In the meantime, perhaps you'll consider reading one of my thriller series? Have you tried the DI Kayli Bright series yet?

Here's the link to the first in the series **The Missing Children**

Thank you for your support as always.
    M A Comley

Reviews are a fantastic way of reaching out and showing an author how much you appreciate their work – so leave one today, if you will.

Printed in Poland
by Amazon Fulfillment
Poland Sp. z o.o., Wrocław